Jacob looked around the garden.

Rebecca could almost see the gears churning in his brain.

"You don't approve?" she asked a bit testily.

"I didn't say that. It's just that I have some ideas I'd like to try."

"Well, maybe you should build a different garden space, then, and leave this one alone." Her voice was tart. So much for a cooperative attitude. She felt protective about the garden and didn't appreciate Jacob's implication that it was subpar.

"Maybe I will." In turn, Jacob's voice was frosty, and the look he gave her was far from benevolent.

She sighed. "I'm sorry, Jacob. That was rude of me. It bothers me to think you don't find it acceptable."

"I didn't say it wasn't acceptable. I simply said I have some ideas I'd like to try. Don't you think that's normal for a new landowner?"

"*Ja* sure, I suppose." She kicked at a small stone at her feet. "I guess I'm wondering if I'll still have a role to play in your new farm, that's all."

He shrugged noncommittally. "That remains to be seen."

Living on a remote self-sufficient homestead in North Idaho, **Patrice Lewis** is a Christian wife, mother, author, blogger, columnist and speaker. She has practiced and written about rural subjects for almost thirty years. When she isn't writing, Patrice enjoys self-sufficiency projects, such as animal husbandry, small-scale dairy production, gardening, food preservation and canning, and homeschooling. She and her husband have been married since 1990 and have two daughters.

Books by Patrice Lewis

Love Inspired

The Amish Newcomer
Amish Baby Lessons
Her Path to Redemption
The Amish Animal Doctor
The Mysterious Amish Nanny
Their Road to Redemption
The Amish Midwife's Bargain
The Amish Beekeeper's Dilemma

Visit the Author Profile page at LoveInspired.com.

The Amish Beekeeper's Dilemma

Patrice Lewis

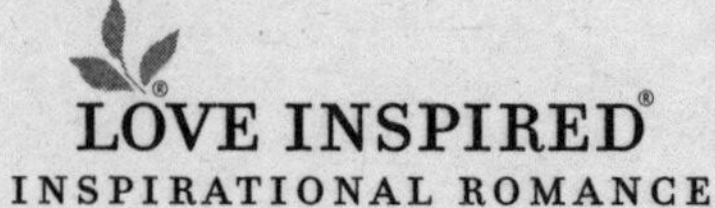

ISBN-13: 978-1-335-59721-2

The Amish Beekeeper's Dilemma

For questions and comments about the quality of this book, please contact us at CustomerService@Harlequin.com.

Love Inspired
22 Adelaide St. West, 41st Floor
Toronto, Ontario M5H 4E3, Canada
www.LoveInspired.com

Printed in U.S.A.

Ye shall inherit their land,
and I will give it unto you to possess it,
a land that floweth with milk and honey.
—*Leviticus* 20:24

To my husband and daughters,
my greatest earthly joy.

To Jesus, for His redeeming grace.

To God, Who has blessed me
more than I could possibly deserve.

Chapter One

Rebecca Hilty, wearing elbow-length gloves and a bee veil over her head, stood in the middle of the clearing and smiled. Honeybees buzzed around her on an otherwise quiet May afternoon. But the bees were not inclined to bother her even after opening several hives and splitting the insects to make new colonies. They were simply getting resettled. She lingered by the hives, enjoying the hum and movement of the insects.

It was a warm day, and the sun shone through the branches of the pine and fir trees that lined the edge of the clearing where her hives were located. It was perfect weather for the task she had just completed: splitting hives. Of the forty-six hives in her bee yard, she had deemed eight of them strong enough to split. Into empty hive boxes, she moved frames thick with developing bees, pollen and capped honey, as well as a queen bee or the resources to make a queen.

If all the splits were successful, she would end up with fifty-four hives instead of forty-six.

She might have been anxious about the actual procedure, but she made sure to display no nervousness around the bees themselves. The insects were quick to detect agitation, and Rebecca had long ago learned never to disturb the colonies if her mood was not calm and unruffled. Somehow, bees knew the difference between an attack from a predator and manipulation by a beekeeper. She was seldom stung.

She considered honeybees one of *Gott*'s most fascinating creatures. She'd been a beekeeper for five years, and this was her second year turning a profit from sales of honey. Her employer and mentor, Caleb Graber, had been completely encouraging when she first expressed interest. Bees were always useful on a farm, he'd told her.

Five years ago, freshly arrived in the new Amish settlement outside the small town of Pierce, Montana, she'd known no one—not even the older man whose advertisement for a farm hand she had boldly answered before she'd moved across the country. Desperate to leave her matchmaking mother and aunt behind, Rebecca had fled her hometown in Indiana and traveled to this new community.

Working for Caleb had been nothing but a joy. She preferred her independence over marriage, and now—at twenty-eight years old—her mother despaired of her ever finding a husband.

Rebecca didn't care. She preferred it here in Montana. Her beekeeping venture was turning into a profitable one at last.

Just then she heard a noise, and turned to see Caleb returning from the bus station in town, directing his horse and buggy toward the barn with a man sitting on the seat beside him.

Normally, the sight of Caleb returning from town was something she looked forward to, but today he was bringing home the great-nephew who was his heir. Rebecca couldn't help but feel resentment over the arrival of someone who would upset the operation of the farm she and Caleb had worked so hard to establish.

She sighed and stripped off her gloves, then removed her bee veil. Her calm mood fled, replaced with gut-clenching nerves. She couldn't avoid meeting the visitor.

Truth be told, deep down she had hoped *she* would be the older man's designated heir. Widowed and childless, Caleb Graber had come to Montana after his wife passed away and started a small farm. When he needed help, he'd put an ad in *The Budget* seeking a farm hand, and she had responded. It had been a perfect match. And she had grown to love Caleb like a *grossdaddi*.

But now…well, now there would be an outsider on the farm who would disturb the harmonious working relationship she and Caleb had established: his brother's grandson from Ohio, who would inherit the farm when it came time for Caleb to retire. His name was Jacob Graber, and Rebecca decided she didn't like him for the simple reason that she didn't want him here. Jacob had never seen the farm, had never had a farm of his own and had never been to Montana, yet she—as the hired hand—would be expected to defer to his inexperience. It grated on her nerves.

Unwilling to jeopardize her warm relationship with

Caleb, she had kept her thoughts to herself. But now she would be forced to be civil toward this…interloper.

Sighing, she first stopped at the small outbuilding Caleb had retrofitted into a cabin for her. She dropped off her bee veil and gloves, then washed her hands. She patted stray strands of hair back beneath her *kapp* and smoothed down her apron. Best to get it over with. She headed toward the main farmhouse.

She saw Caleb holding one suitcase, while the other man held two more. They were carrying them from the barn, where the buggy was stored, toward the house.

"Ah, Rebecca, there you are!" Caleb smiled. "I'd like you to meet my great-nephew Jacob Graber. Jacob, this is Rebecca Hilty, my right-hand helper."

She approached as Jacob put the suitcases on the ground. *"Guder nammidaag,"* she said, smiling through gritted teeth as she held out her hand.

"Guder nammidaag," he repeated. His smile seemed no more genuine than hers, his chin was lifted with a touch of haughtiness, and his handshake was firm—almost too firm, as if he was testing her strength. "Caleb has talked about you the whole way home."

Jacob had curly brown hair and dark blue eyes with laugh wrinkles at the corners. He looked tired—understandable after his cross-country trip—and she noticed his smile didn't quite reach his eyes.

For whatever reason, it seemed Jacob was no more thrilled to meet her than she was to meet him.

She dropped his hand and turned to Caleb, who seemed oblivious of the undercurrents of tension between her and Jacob. "That pot of lentil soup I put on after lunch has been simmering all afternoon. All I have to do is bake the biscuits I cut out earlier and dinner should be ready. While they're baking, I'll do the evening chores."

"Ja gut," Caleb replied. "It will give Jacob a chance to get settled in the house." With a spryness belying his seventy-two years, Caleb reached again for the suitcase at his feet, while Jacob picked up the remaining two and followed the older man indoors without a backward glance.

Thinning her lips, Rebecca stepped into the cheerful sage-and-cream kitchen she and Caleb had painted shortly after her arrival. She remained just long enough to slide the biscuits into the oven and snatch up the egg basket, then fled toward the sanctity of the barn.

In the building's shadowy interior, she pressed a hand to her chest and took a calming breath. Her first impression of Jacob was not positive. Though barely exchanging a greeting, she'd picked up overtones of arrogance that rankled her, and her inclination to dislike him deepened.

But she didn't want to hurt Caleb's feelings, which meant she would be forced to work with Jacob, interact with him, while pretending his very presence didn't threaten her place on the farm she had come to love so well.

If nothing else, he couldn't complain about her efficiency. In the twenty minutes it took the biscuits to bake, she fed the chickens, gathered up the eggs, tucked the calves into their pen for the night and made sure the horses and cows had fresh water. They did not need extra food this time of year, with the pastures so lush and green.

When she could no longer find an excuse to linger in the barn, she picked up the egg basket and headed back to the house, where she found Caleb had already set the kitchen table. Jacob sat with a cup of coffee at his elbow, and listened to the older man's cheerful chatter.

"Everything snug in the barn?" Caleb inquired.

"Ja," she said shortly. She turned to wash her hands, then pulled the biscuits from the oven.

"Rebecca makes the world's best biscuits," Caleb said into the yawning silence. "Even better than my wife's, and that's saying a lot. Jacob, do you want another cup of coffee?"

"Nein, danke." Jacob knuckled his eyes. "I don't want anything to keep me from a good night's sleep. It's been a long trip."

"I can imagine. You'll feel better in the morning. Rebecca can walk you around the farm and show you everything we've accomplished in the past five years. I think you'll be impressed."

"I'm sure I will. *Danke*," he added as Rebecca set the pot of soup on a hot pad in the center of the table.

She piled the biscuits in a cloth-lined bowl and snatched up a small tub containing homemade butter, and brought them to the table as well.

She paused, along with Jacob and Caleb, for a silent blessing over the food. The men might be expressing thanks for the food. Rebecca found herself praying for peace of mind and forbearance during what she saw as a difficult time ahead.

Sometimes, she knew, silence was golden. When she worked with the bees, she was forced to move calmly and without agitation. She would borrow a page from her apiary duties and apply it toward the newcomer.

One thing was certain: she saw no reason to be any more pleasant to Jacob than common courtesy demanded. She wouldn't be rude; she wouldn't be argumentative. She would just be…quiet.

Four days of traveling by train and bus from Ohio to Montana had left Jacob Graber exhausted. Sitting upright on public transportation seats rather than reclining in a proper bed would do that to a person. He was delighted to see Caleb, but his great-uncle was inclined to be sociable and chatty, and Jacob was almost too dazed to pay attention.

And then there was Rebecca. On the way from the bus station to the farm, Caleb had waxed eloquent about his hired hand. Personally he would have thought it better to hire a man, but whatever. Jacob had a mental image of an amazon of a woman. If she was still unmarried at her age—Caleb had said she was twenty-eight, the same age as himself—then she must not be much to look at, though clearly Caleb thought she had other qualities to admire.

The reality was far different than he imagined. She was slim and tidy, attired in a forest green dress and black apron. Her white *kapp* was perched neatly atop her dark brown hair. Her brown eyes looked wary. She had a dusting of freckles across her nose, and a steel set to her jaw.

In short, she looked nothing like he'd envisioned her. She wasn't an amazon; she was somewhat tall and rawboned, he realized, but not to the point of plainness. She wasn't pretty, but she looked like she had character.

She did, however, give every impression of being a stubborn woman who wouldn't lightly release the reins of control she had on the farm.

The food was superb—a hearty lentil soup with plenty of ham, and flaky biscuits that were so delicious he polished off half a dozen—but Rebecca barely said a word.

To him she seemed positively sulky. She kept her eyes on the bowl in front of her and rarely lifted them, even when Caleb addressed her directly.

He watched her as he ate the soup. Privately, Jacob wondered why Caleb hadn't designated Rebecca as his heir, rather than himself. The old man seemed to think the world of the woman. But however his great-uncle had decided to pass the farm along to him, Jacob was beyond grateful.

Because Jacob wanted a farm…badly. As was customary among the Amish, his younger brother had inherited the family farm. His older brother had managed to purchase his own farm. But as the middle son, Jacob felt rootless and unanchored. Land prices in Ohio were high, property was scarce, and for the past eight years he had worked on his older brother's land.

This left Jacob in too precarious a financial position to consider courting a wife or starting a family. He felt like he was in limbo, and was growing increasingly frustrated under his older brother's tutelage and unable to implement some of the farming practices he wanted to try.

So Caleb's offer to pass on his farm to him was an enormous blessing. For this reason, Jacob was willing to be patient with the old man's chatter, even as he fought to keep his eyes open.

"You said the farm is fifty acres?" he inserted at one point.

"*Ja.* About half in forest, the other half in pasture." Caleb stroked his wispy beard in a thoughtful gesture. "There's a lot of clay in the soil. It's hard work plowing for grain. Plowing is one thing I do better than Rebecca, and to be honest I won't mind turning it over to a younger man."

"Why do you grow grain if it's too hard?" inquired Jacob.

Caleb looked startled. "It's what I've always done," he replied in a puzzled voice.

It was one of the things Jacob hoped to change—how the land responded to farming practices. If the soil had too much clay to plow for grain, perhaps growing grain wasn't the best thing to do.

But it was too early in his reacquaintance with Caleb to offer criticism or suggest improvements. When the farm was fully under his control, Jacob would be free to implement all the ideas he wanted to try. Ideas, he thought sourly, that his brother Nathan refused to consider, no matter how persuasive Jacob made his arguments.

Through dinner, Rebecca remained silent. He knew she was listening intently to the conversation between him and Caleb, but she said not a word. Her face was expressionless.

After dinner, Rebecca excused herself to wash dishes,

then murmured, *"Gude nacht,"* and disappeared so abruptly that Caleb stared after her.

"The hired hand doesn't seem to like me," Jacob remarked to Caleb.

"What on earth's gotten into her?" murmured Caleb, his expression full of confusion.

"Whatever it is, I'm too tired to worry about it." Jacob punctuated his words with a huge yawn. "I hope you don't mind if I go to bed early."

"*Ja* sure." His uncle flapped a hand. "Your bed's all made up. Sleep as long as you need to."

"I will, *danke*." Jacob leaned over and kissed him on the cheek. "I'm very glad to be here, Uncle Caleb. It's so *gut* to see you again."

His uncle blushed and flapped a hand again. "Go on, get some sleep."

Jacob washed up a bit, then pulled out his nightclothes from one of the suitcases. He was almost too tired to appreciate the sound of crickets coming through the screened window, or the hooting of a great horned owl in a distant tree. He slid between the sheets, murmured his evening prayers and closed his eyes.

The only thought that crossed his mind before he dropped off to sleep was mild annoyance at Rebecca's blatant antipathy. He didn't much care. Once Caleb returned to Ohio, as he planned, it might be best for all parties involved if Rebecca could be eased into another job somewhere else.

Chapter Two

In the morning, Rebecca left her cabin to go about her usual chores, starting with milking the cows. She knew she had been rude last night, and it pricked her conscience a little. It wasn't Jacob's fault that Caleb didn't leave the farm to her.

She sat on the milking stool, thinking through her dilemma, when a quiet voice interrupted her. "Rebecca?"

She turned around and saw Caleb standing behind her. *"Ja? Guder mariye."*

"*Guder mariye. Liebling*, is everything *oll recht*? You were so quiet last night. Jacob is convinced it's because you don't like him."

Guilt flared again. Rebecca turned back to the cow and pressed her forehead into the animal's flank as she continued milking. "*Ja*, I'm sorry about that."

"But *why* don't you like him?" the older man persisted. "You only just met him."

Not for anything would Rebecca admit her secret hope to inherit the farm, and her bitterness at being overlooked. "Women have moods," she lied. "It's nothing more than that."

She could sense Caleb doubted her excuse, but he didn't question her further. Instead, he gave a noncommittal grunt and went to feed the chickens.

When she finished milking the cows, Rebecca released the animals into the pasture and seized the milk buckets. She braced herself for the inevitable interaction with Jacob in the kitchen of the main house. *Just be polite*, she told herself.

Sure enough, he was seated at the kitchen table, nursing a cup of coffee and glancing at the latest issue of *The Budget*. He raised his head when she stepped inside. *"Guder mariye."*

"Guder mariye," she replied. Aware that she was being watched, she began making breakfast, her movements efficient. While the bacon was frying, she strained the fresh milk, put the jars into the icebox and removed yesterday's milk to skim the cream.

The tasks were ordinary, yet Rebecca felt her cheeks heat. She wasn't used to an audience.

"You don't say much, do you?" Jacob observed sardonically.

"Nein," she replied.

He gave a small snort of what sounded like amusement, and returned to his newspaper.

A few minutes later, thankfully, Caleb entered the kitchen with a basket of eggs, breaking the tension. "*Guder mariye*, Jacob," he said. "How did you sleep?"

"Like a rock. I was so tired last night."

"I can imagine." The older man took plates out of

the cabinet and began setting the table, as was his usual custom.

"Breakfast is almost ready," Rebecca said, taking a few of the fresh eggs and cracking them into a frying pan. Within a few minutes, the meal was ready.

After the blessing, she helped herself to bacon and eggs while Caleb outlined the day ahead. "I think the first thing to do is have Rebecca show you around," he said to Jacob. "She knows the property almost better than I do." He smiled at her. "She's the one who helped make this farm a reality after my wife passed away. Couldn't have done it without her."

His praise was not unusual, and Rebecca smiled automatically at her dear friend. But deep down, she wondered why—if she was so valued—he had decided to shift his legacy from her to Jacob.

"*Danke*, I would like to see the whole property," said Jacob, biting into a piece of crispy bacon. "I have some ideas I wanted to implement on my brother's farm that I never had a chance to do, and it will be interesting to see if they'll work here."

Rebecca saw a shadow of doubt creep into Caleb's face. "Well, we just got the farm showing a profit," he replied on a warning note. "You may not want to make too many changes that the profit disappears."

"*Nein*, of course not, Uncle. But there has been some noteworthy new research on farming techniques that caught my interest a few years ago."

"Rebecca can help you out. I'll be heading into town this morning to drop some butter and eggs at Yoder's Mercantile to sell, and to meet Ephraim for coffee."

Ephraim King was one of Caleb's best friends, and the two often met in town.

"And I'll make more butter this afternoon," Rebecca said. She forked up the last of her eggs, then rose to clear her dishes away. She looked at Jacob. "I'll be in my cabin until you're ready for the tour." After nodding at Caleb, she slipped out the kitchen door.

But she didn't go straight to her cabin. Instead, she went to the bee yard and sat on a log near the edge, absorbing the atmosphere of the industrious insects and praying for peace of mind. She couldn't shake the worry that Jacob's presence here would ultimately lead to her dismissal. Five years' worth of work would go down the drain.

A bee landed on her hand. Rebecca lifted the insect to eye level and watched as it walked delicately on her wrist, exploring. When it was clear the bee would not be finding any pollen on her hand, it lifted off and darted away.

She followed it with her eyes. Honeybees were wonders of creation, cooperating as a colony in ways that still mystified human researchers.

Whereas she couldn't even seem to cooperate with Jacob.

Feeling chastened, she rose from the log, dusted off her skirt and headed for her cabin. For Caleb's sake, she could at least stop sulking and get along with Jacob. If nothing else, perhaps he would be less inclined to tell her he no longer needed her services. Then she could continue to work this land that she had come to love so well.

Until he stopped by, she occupied herself trimming

some of the deadwood from the herbs she had planted in beds near her front door. The air smelled pungent with sage when she saw him walking over.

"Ready for a tour?" she asked.

He seemed almost surprised to be addressed directly. *"Ja,"* he replied.

"Then let's go." She placed the trimmers near the door and led the way toward the barn.

The structure was large and solid, built at least fifty years ago. "This was here when Caleb bought the property," she began. "The house and barn, the cabin I'm staying in and the chicken coop were already here, but that was about it. Not much by way of fencing, no garden, no field crops. Just buildings."

"What kinds of animals does Caleb keep?" asked Jacob, glancing around at the large old-fashioned structure. "Horses, cows, what else?"

"He has three Jersey cows and calves, four pigs and a flock of perhaps twenty chickens. That's it except the horses—two draft and two buggy horses."

"Does he cut his own hay?"

"*Ja.* It took a bit to get the fields into decent shape, but he's self-sufficient in animal feed at the moment."

Jacob gave a small grunt of approval. At least she hoped it was approval. It had taken a long time to improve the hay fields, so she hoped he appreciated the amount of work that went into them.

She showed him the pigpen, the horse stalls, the cow pens, calf pens, milking stall and other infrastructure. He didn't say much, just peered into corners and nodded at the fencing she and Caleb had installed. It was a typical Amish smallholding, nothing she was sure Jacob hadn't seen his whole life.

Then they approached a small cornfield. "I'll admit, it's been a struggle growing corn here, since the rainfall patterns and soil conditions are much different than Indiana or Ohio," she said.

"Why doesn't Caleb do what the land is telling him?"

Rebecca peered at him, confused. "What do you mean?"

"Never mind." He waved a hand dismissively. "Keep going with the tour, *bitte*."

"*Ja* sure." Rebecca strode toward an enclosure with netting extending to ten feet in height.

"This is the garden." Next to the beehives, the garden was her pride and joy. "We have a lot of deer and elk in the area, so tall fences are necessary."

"Why is it all in raised beds?" inquired Jacob, following her through the gate.

"The soil has too much clay," she replied. "Throughout the settlement, we quickly learned it was easier to grow in raised beds than in the ground."

"Could the soil be amended?"

"*Ja* sure, but it would be a constant battle. Raised beds work fine." Rebecca was proud of the garden. The beds were tidy rectangles, made with pressure-treated lumber and old tin siding, watered with a drip irrigation system, and highly productive. "We have plenty of food to put up for the winter for ourselves, and we sell a lot of the extra produce at Yoder's Mercantile in town."

"I see." Jacob looked around the garden, and Rebecca could almost see the gears churning in his brain.

"You don't approve?" she asked a bit testily.

"I didn't say that. It's just that I have some ideas I'd like to try."

"Well, maybe you should build a different garden space, then, and leave this one alone." Her voice was tart. So much for a cooperative attitude. She felt protective about the garden, and didn't appreciate Jacob's implication that it was subpar.

"Maybe I will." In turn, Jacob's voice was frosty, and the look he gave her was far from benevolent.

She sighed. "I'm sorry, Jacob, that was rude of me. To be truthful, the garden was a great deal of hard work, and now it's quite a success. It bothers me to think you don't find it acceptable."

"I didn't say it wasn't acceptable. I simply said I have some ideas I'd like to try. Don't you think that's normal for a new landowner?"

"*Ja* sure, I suppose." She kicked at a small stone at her feet. "I guess I'm wondering if I'll still have a role to play in your new farm, that's all."

He shrugged noncommittally. "That remains to be seen."

To Rebecca, he may as well have fired her on the spot. She could see the handwriting on the wall. She turned away. "Follow me and I'll show you the stock pond and the woodlot."

She pointed out amenities and improvements, but her mind was flopping this way and that. She sensed her time on the farm would soon come to an end. Next Sunday after church, she would begin making discreet inquiries for another position. She knew what her mother would say if she was aware of Rebecca's imminent dismissal: *It's high time you got married. What's taking you so long?* Her mother's view was that marriage solved everything.

But whether or not she had a future here on Jacob's farm, marriage wasn't for her. Her mother had tried to push her down that path, and the result had been humiliating. It was far easier to simply look for another job.

On the whole, Jacob approved of what he saw on the farm. Caleb had accomplished a lot in the five years he'd worked this land, and clearly tried to model this property after the small farms in the Midwest.

He understood why growing large fields of corn was problematic. Before arriving in Montana, Jacob had done research on what kind of growing conditions he could expect, and a water-intensive crop like corn wasn't on the list in an area that saw dry summers.

But Jacob had become interested in an alternative style of farming called permaculture, and it differed in many ways from traditional Amish farming practices. If Caleb indeed retired back to his old hometown in Ohio, then implementing new plans wouldn't be a problem… except for Rebecca.

Clearly, the woman was protective of what she and Caleb had accomplished, and didn't seem open to the new plans Jacob wanted to try.

"Here's the stock pond." Her quiet voice interrupted his thoughts. "It's fed by runoff and hasn't gone dry in the five years I've been here."

The small body of water was ringed on half its perimeter by tall conifers and had a low earth dam at the far end. He scanned the area, noting the slope of the land and how it funneled water naturally into the pond. "See, this is something I plan to improve," he commented. "Since Montana is drier than Ohio, managing rainwater flow is an important part of permaculture."

"What's permaculture?" ventured Rebecca.

"It's an agricultural system that mixes human activity with natural surroundings. In a nutshell, it creates self-sustaining systems to produce crops with far less work than conventional farming techniques."

Rebecca wrinkled her brow. "Farming is always work."

"*Ja* sure, of course. But it doesn't necessarily have to be the never-ending backbreaking toil we've been taught." He could feel himself warming to his favorite subject. "One of the things I want to try on this farm is incorporating some of the theories I've read about in hopes of making things easier in the long run. It's not a fast process, but I believe it will be a satisfying one." He scanned the woods, the pond, the rim of sedge grasses near the water. "Water is an important part of the process. One of the things I'd like to do is create another pond in a different location, depending on the lay of the land. But I'm pleased to see one pond already in place."

"It was here when Caleb bought the land. Where else would you want to put a pond?"

"I don't know yet. It will take some study. This sounds funny to say, but I have to figure out where a pond wants to be."

She shrugged. "Seems silly to take a system that already works, like we've established here, and change it."

"Maybe so, but the long-term goal is to make things easier. One way is to plant what the land can support. If the soil has too much clay and the climate is too dry, then corn is not a *gut* choice to plant. What might be better are crops such as wheat or oats."

"*Ja*, many people grow grain crops here," she admitted. "And that's why we garden in raised beds."

Jacob didn't want to get too deep into theory at the moment, especially with someone who didn't know much about the subject. But then Rebecca said something that floored him.

"Now I'll show you the bee yard," she said, turning away from the pond.

Jacob stood rooted for a moment. "Bee yard?" he repeated. "Caleb has bees?"

For the first time he saw pleasure flicker across Rebecca's face, an expression that instantly turned her from ordinary into extraordinary. Her strong face softened, her eyes grew soft, and for a moment, she looked almost pretty.

"Ja," she replied. "Just yesterday, when Caleb was picking you up from the bus station in town, I was splitting hives. If all the splits are successful, that means we have fifty-four hives now."

Honeybees were an integral part of the permaculture system he wanted to implement. What a blessing to have them already in place! "Show me," he said eagerly.

She led the way to a clearing a short distance from her cabin. Dozens of hive boxes painted in various pastel colors were arranged in a loose circle. A large log rested near the edge.

"These are the hives I split," she said, gesturing toward a cluster. "I've been selecting for colonies that seem to have a natural resistance to varroa mites."

"Mites," he remarked. "Those are bad, *ja*?"

"*Ja*. They're an invasive parasite that is now present in almost every hive in the world. They bring diseases, too, so hives that can resist the mites are valuable. The hives I split yesterday were strong and doing a *gut* job of resisting."

He stood still, absorbing the activity and hum of the insects. Rebecca stood silently beside him.

Honeybees. They represented more than just the obvious benefits of honey. They were a valuable addition to his plans for the farm and its pollination needs.

"Caleb was smart," he murmured. "I'm glad the bees are here."

He saw Rebecca stiffen. "Caleb isn't the one who works them," she snapped. "I am."

"Then you'll have to teach me what you know."

She turned away. "If I feel like it." She spoke under her breath so quietly as to be almost inaudible.

But he heard. Annoyance rippled through him. She seemed determined to defy him at every opportunity. "Fine," he snapped back. "I can learn on my own."

Before she could respond, Caleb's buggy came into view, the horse's hooves clip-clopping up the gravel driveway. With relief, Jacob turned his back on Rebecca and went to meet the older man.

"What do you think of the farm?" Caleb asked cheerfully. He pulled the horse to a stop.

"It's *wunnerschee*," replied Jacob with a smile. He wasn't about to admit to the tension between him and

Rebecca. "You've done a tremendous amount of work in five years."

"*Ja*, but that's the biggest word. *Work.* I'm ready to hand things off to a younger man." Caleb climbed down from the buggy with a dexterity that belied his age.

"Well, I'm more grateful than I can say. I'll go unhitch." Jacob took the bridle of the horse and led it into the barn, where he unhitched the animal, gave it a brief grooming and released it into the field with the other horses.

Caleb lingered in the barn during these chores. "Did Rebecca show you the garden?" he asked. "And the pond? And the grain fields?"

"*Ja*, she showed me everything." Jacob smiled at his uncle's enthusiasm. "Including the beehives. I must admit, those really caught my attention. What a blessing to have so much pollination so close by."

"Rebecca is the one who does all the work with them," the older man admitted. "I've called her the 'bee whisperer' because she never seems to get stung."

"Do you have much honey to sell?" Jacob hooked the bridle on the peg indicated, then followed Caleb toward the house.

"More each year. Last fall we brought in a total of five gallons or so, packed in quart jars, to sell at Yoder's Mercantile in town. That's not counting what we sell directly to church members." Caleb glanced at Jacob. "Did, ah, Rebecca seem friendlier this morning?"

Jacob debated for a few moments, then decided on the truth. "*Nein.* I don't know what her problem is, but she just doesn't seem to want me here. To be honest,

Uncle Caleb, I don't know if she's going to want to keep working on the farm once you return to Ohio."

"She feels very…possessive about the place," Caleb said, opening the screen door to the kitchen. Jacob followed. "Some coffee?"

"Ja, bitte." Jacob removed his hat and hung it on a hook near the door as his uncle poured some of the morning's remaining coffee from a thermos into two mugs. "Possessiveness is one thing," he remarked. "But jealousy is another. That's what I think she suffers from."

"Of you?"

Jacob turned, startled. Rebecca stood just outside the screen door, a basket of cut herbs in her hands. Her eyes flashed with anger.

"You think I'm jealous of *you*?" she repeated, a thread of fury in her voice. "Why don't you just admit you don't want me here and be done with it?" She whirled so fast, some of the herbs went flying. She dashed down the pathway toward her cabin.

Stunned silence followed in her wake as both Jacob and Caleb stared after her.

"I think," Caleb began after a moment, "it's time I ease these troubled waters."

"Do you think it will help?" Jacob tried to keep the cynicism from his voice as he dropped into one of the kitchen chairs. "Tell me, Uncle, would you be terribly upset if I let Rebecca go?"

Concern filled the older man's face. "*Ja*, I would be upset!" he exclaimed. "She's like a granddaughter to me!"

"*Ja* sure, but she seems to hate my guts, for whatever reason." Jacob toyed with the handle of his mug. "I don't know how much I can get done if she's going to butt heads with me all hours of the day."

"I'll talk to her," Caleb said. "To be honest, I've never seen her this way. For five years, she's worked hard and cheerfully. Why would all that change in so short a time?"

A thought struck Jacob, but he didn't voice it. Was Rebecca upset because Caleb had willed the farm to him? Had she expected it would go to her? An even darker idea struck him: Was her long association with Caleb purely mercenary? Had she worked for his uncle solely for the purpose of inheriting the farm?

It would help to explain her otherwise inexplicable hostility.

But Caleb was troubled enough by Rebecca's outburst, and he didn't want to add to the older man's burdens.

"Well, we haven't even known each other for twenty-four hours," he said, being somewhat evasive. "I'm sure she'll come around."

"I hope so." Caleb still looked troubled. "I don't want her to leave. I hope you two can get along after I return to Ohio."

In Jacob's mind, what Caleb didn't know wouldn't hurt him. After the older man returned to Ohio, he would have the freedom to do what he liked on the farm, including hiring—or firing—employees.

But he'd worry about that later. Right now he would focus on trying to get along with Rebecca.

Chapter Three

The momentary lesson on cooperation from the bees hadn't lasted long. Rebecca reflected with grim humor that bees were smarter than humans in some respect. As always, during times of trouble, she found herself sitting on the log at the edge of the bee yard, trying to calm herself.

So Jacob thought she was jealous of him, did he? Maybe he was right. She wiped away an angry tear and considered the unfairness of life.

The trouble with moving off this property was she had nowhere to go. Sure, someone in the church community would rent her a room or a cabin, and she could undoubtedly find a job somewhere, but what about her beloved beehives? They weren't exactly portable.

Three feet or three miles. That was the rule of thumb when moving hives. If a hive was moved even a few yards from its previous location, the bees became confused because the landmarks by which they navigated were altered. If a hive needed to be moved, it was far better to move it a longer distance away and let the bees start afresh.

Besides, hives full of brood and honey were heavy. Most *Englischers* used forklifts or tractors if it was necessary to move active hives from one location to another. She had nothing but herself.

If Jacob fired her, she wasn't about to leave behind her colonies. They were hers, and hers alone.

The other alternative was to return home to Indiana, but that meant returning to her mother and her aunt's obsessive matchmaking. Their last attempt five years ago to find her a husband had been disastrous.

Jeremiah, the young man they wanted her to marry, hadn't been so bad at first. He had courted her with moderate enthusiasm. She'd been moderately interested in return. All seemed to be progressing normally. Her best friend, Leah, had also been courting a young man selected for her by a group of busybody older women whose goal in life was to get every unmarried girl in the community married as quickly as possible.

Then, what seemed like such a promising match turned sour. Jeremiah abruptly abandoned her to pursue a construction job among the *Englisch* with the lame excuse that he wasn't ready to get married yet.

It was a blow to her ego in many respects. It affected her standing in the church community, since many now viewed her with pity. But later, she'd heard through the grapevine the *real* reason for his departure…and that hurt her pride even more. It made her determined to marry only on her own terms.

Her mother promptly started recommending other

men, but Rebecca had balked. No one was going to dictate her romantic future, especially after the fiasco with Jeremiah. When Caleb's advertisement in *The Budget* caught her eye, Rebecca had leaped at the chance to leave Indiana. When he hired her, she attributed it to the hand of *Gott*, and was forever grateful to the older man for offering her an escape from her family.

Her mother and father hadn't been pleased with her decision to move away, but Jeremiah's abandonment had tapped into a wellspring of independence Rebecca never knew she had. She moved anyway.

But now, that might all be coming to an end. Rebecca stared glumly at her hives, watching the intense, focused activity of the insects.

Bees didn't sting unless they were threatened. Maybe that's why she was "stinging" Jacob—she felt threatened. She'd felt that same level of threat when her mother offered to match her with another man after Jeremiah left. She realized she was afraid to leave this farm—not because of any concerns for her safety, but because she had come to love this land with a fierceness and, yes, a sense of possessiveness.

She sighed and stood up. She was neglecting her chores sitting here and sulking among the bees.

She'd told Caleb she would make butter this afternoon. It was possible to make the butter in her own cabin, though it meant fetching the cream from the main house and possibly running into Jacob there. Lifting her chin, Rebecca entered the kitchen and was thankful no one was in sight. She raided the icebox, packed jars of cream into a crate and prepared to carry the crate to her cabin.

Just then, Caleb walked into the kitchen. "Rebecca, *liebling*, we need to talk."

Her stomach clenched in a knot of dread. She set down the crate on the kitchen table. *"Ja?"*

"What's wrong?"

She countered with her own question. "Where's Jacob?"

"He's pulling together some lumber in the barn for a project he wants to try. Now tell me, what's wrong? It's not normal for you to be so out of sorts."

She kept her eyes on the crate full of jars. "I don't know how to answer that, Caleb. But for some reason, Jacob just rubs me the wrong way."

"Has he said anything inappropriate?"

"Nein..."

The older man tugged at his wispy white beard. "My concern is that he may not want to keep you around after I leave Montana. He said as much to me."

"*Ja*, he said as much to me, too." Rebecca felt remorseful at how worried her mentor looked. "I'm sorry, Caleb. I'll try harder to be pleasant."

"*Ja*, that might be best. I'm worried about you, *liebling*." He paused. "When I travel back to Ohio, do you want to accompany me? It's not far from my hometown to yours. You could return to your family."

"Nein." Caleb knew the reason why she had fled Indiana and accepted his job offer in Montana.

"Then how about you live near me in Ohio? At least it's an option."

Her heart swelled with fondness for the grandfatherly figure. Caleb had always looked out for her. "*Danke*, Caleb." She leaned over and kissed him on the cheek. "It's *gut* to know I have choices if—if I have to leave here." She looked at the crate full of jars of cream and changed her mind about making butter in her cabin. She was used to making it here in the main house anyway. "I suppose I'll start by not actively avoiding Jacob."

Caleb left to work elsewhere, and Rebecca went about warming the cream and pouring it into the churn. She was cranking the handle when Jacob came into the kitchen.

He stopped short when he saw her. "Where's Caleb?" he inquired.

"I don't know." She kept turning the crank and decided it was time to be direct. "Is this going to work, Jacob?"

"Is *what* going to work?"

"Having me here, doing the same job I've been doing for five years."

He was silent, and she risked a glance at him. He looked like he had eaten a lemon.

"I don't know," he responded at last. "All I know is you've treated me like a pariah since the moment I arrived, before I'd even said two words to you."

Shame drenched her. "*Ja*, I know." She couldn't or wouldn't admit why. "But Caleb knocked some sense into my head a few minutes ago, bless him. He basically told me I'd better mend my ways or you wouldn't waste any time kicking me out."

Wary admiration lit up his face. "He's as blunt as I

remember," he said in a musing voice. "What a pity he and Aunt Naomi never could have children. He'd have been an outstanding father."

"He's been like a grandfather to me all these years," she admitted. "And sometimes it takes an older and wiser person to tell a younger one when they're misbehaving. So I suppose I owe you an apology."

He raised his eyebrows. "So why were you so hostile from the start?"

She kept her eyes on the butter churn while her hands continued to turn the crank. "Let's just say that's my own business."

"If I could hazard a guess, I might say it's because you hoped Caleb would leave the farm to *you*."

She jerked up her head, knowing her expression betrayed her.

Sure enough, Jacob nodded. "I thought so."

"You're making a lot of assumptions."

"Actually, I think it's no longer an assumption, but a fact. Admit it, Rebecca, you thought you'd inherit the farm."

"*Ja* sure. Caleb and I have worked closely for five years and he's always treated me like a member of the family. He has no children. Tell me why I was wrong to think he would provide this farm as my legacy."

He shrugged. "I can't answer that. All I know is that I don't feel guilty over his decision, but I do feel gratitude."

"You didn't know in advance?"

"*Nein*. It was completely out of the blue. A gift from *Gott*, in my opinion."

She resumed churning the butter. "Well, your gain is

my loss." She decided on a bit more honesty. "I've come to love this farm as no other spot on Earth, in part because I've put so much blood, sweat and tears into it."

"And you want to stay." It was a statement more than a question.

"Ja," she replied. "Of course I want to stay."

He rubbed his chin. "To be frank, I'm waiting for Caleb to go back east before I make some of the more drastic changes I want to try."

"Drastic changes?" she exclaimed. "What kind of drastic changes? The farm is in excellent shape!"

His face shuttered. "I'm not going to go into that right now. I'll admit, however, you and Caleb have done wonders in five years."

She refused to feel placated. "Be that as it may, you have no right…" Her voice trailed off.

He shot her a sour look. "No right to what? Make changes?"

"I didn't say that. Oh, look, the cream is turning." Grains of butter made the churning more difficult.

Jacob did an about-face and stalked out of the kitchen.

Rebecca dropped onto a kitchen chair and rested her chin on her hands. She'd done it again. What was it about Jacob that brought out the absolute worst in her? Why couldn't she keep a civil tongue in her head?

Yes, at the next church service, it seemed best to discreetly inquire about the possibility of a new place to live.

What made that woman tick? Jacob strode toward the barn and the project he had been working on earlier, scowling at a perfectly innocent fence post. Did she honestly think he had no right to make changes to the farm and try out some of his theories?

Her jealousy was unacceptable. Whatever her issues with Caleb's decision about willing the farm to him, she had better get over it right quick.

He entered the barn to continue working on the day's project, and paused as he saw Caleb engaged in tightening some loose hinges on one of the horse stalls. Despite his annoyance at Rebecca's attitude, he couldn't help but smile at his great-uncle's attention to detail.

"What are you working on?" Caleb asked, gesturing toward Jacob's project with a screwdriver.

A low frame of two-by-fours was lying in the center of the barn, with a roll of chicken wire nearby. Jacob was pleased to see abundant building materials tucked in odd nooks and corners of the barn. He had even found a box on a shelf holding an assortment of salvaged casters and small wheels.

"A chicken tractor," he replied.

"A what?" Caleb straightened up.

Jacob chuckled. "It's going to be a low, floorless cage on wheels. I can move it every day and give the chickens fresh things to eat."

"Why would you want to do that?" inquired Caleb. "They're fine in their yard."

"Maybe so, but it's one of the things I want to experiment with—decreasing how much commercial chicken feed they eat and replacing it with what they would eat under less controlled conditions. Their yard is pretty bare right now. I figure if I can move this cage around, it will give the hens new places they can scratch for bugs and insects. They'll act as a mini plow. I have a hankering to try expanding the garden, and this is the first step to doing that—letting the chickens do the work."

"Hmm." Caleb leaned on the stall door. "Need a hand?"

"*Ja* sure!" Jacob was pleased at his uncle's willingness to help.

Together they strengthened the frame, attached some casters to the corners and stretched the chicken wire around the structure, stapling it in place. He also built a hatch door at one end that could lift up and down.

While they worked, Caleb waxed eloquent about the beauties of this corner of Montana. "You'll enjoy meeting the church community," he said, holding the chicken wire in place while Jacob stapled it to the frame. "They're a *gut* group."

"I'm surprised you haven't met a nice older widow and remarried," Jacob teased.

Caleb chuckled, though it held a note of sadness. "*Nein.* I haven't found anyone who could replace my Naomi. She was the only one for me."

Jacob remembered his great-aunt Naomi. She had been a warm and loving woman. Everyone had always thought it was a pity she and Caleb couldn't have children.

"You know, Uncle, there's no need for you to go back to Ohio if you don't want to." He stapled another section of chicken wire to the frame. "I'd be happy to build you a *daadi haus* if you want to stay here."

"Hmm." Caleb stroked his beard, something Jacob

knew he did when he was troubled or thoughtful. "My plans are to go east in a couple of months. My *bruder* and *schwesters* are expecting me."

"I won't try to talk you out of something you truly want to do, but you should be aware you have options."

"Options." Caleb smiled. "That's what I was just discussing with Rebecca today, that she has options ahead of her…if—if you chose not to continue employing her."

Jacob's eyebrows rose. "What kinds of options?"

"She could return to Indiana, to her family."

"That seems like a fine idea." Jacob shrugged.

"*Ja, ja*, but she had a falling-out with her family. I won't say more since it's not my story to tell. So I told her that if she wanted, she could move with me to Ohio, to my old hometown. I wouldn't mind her staying close to me as I get older. I've come to look upon her as a granddaughter."

"So you've said." Jacob felt familiar frustration welling up. "What is it you see in her, Uncle Caleb?"

"*Ach*, where do I begin! She's kind, resourceful and hardworking. She's handy with tools and knows livestock like the back of her hand. She's become well-known for her bees, both here in the Amish settlement and in town. Everyone wants her honey. She has a *gut* head for business, too."

Privately, Jacob thought his uncle was just biased. Apparently, Rebecca had weaseled her way into the older man's heart.

"You just don't know her yet," continued Caleb. "What I suggest is you involve her in all these changes and projects you want to do. It's her job, after all, to be helpful on the farm. Make the most of it. Once you get to know her as I do, I think you'll agree you're better off keeping her on."

Jacob got a distinct impression from his uncle, as if Caleb were pushing him toward Rebecca for more than just business reasons. But perhaps it was only his imagination?

Maybe Caleb was right. If Jacob was stuck with her for the time being, he ought to at least make good use of her. "Maybe I will," he said. "I have an idea I want to try for expanding the garden area. It would certainly be easier with two people instead of one."

"Ja gut." Caleb smiled, and Jacob tried not to read too much into it.

"I think this is ready," he said instead. He knew the structure was a bit heavy, and didn't want to overexert his uncle. "Maybe I should ask Rebecca to help me flip it over and move it into location. She was in the kitchen making butter last I saw."

"I'm heading inside, should I ask her?"

"Ja, bitte."

Caleb departed for the house, and Jacob occupied himself attaching handles to all four sides of the structure for ease of movement. Within a few minutes, Rebecca appeared in the barn door. "Caleb said you wanted to see me?"

He looked at her. Her *kapp* was tidy over her dark hair, but her dark green dress and black apron had a few smudges on them. Her facial expression was neutral.

"Ja," he replied. "I need help flipping this over and thought it might be too heavy for Uncle Caleb."

"What is it?" She came closer.

He went through a similar explanation for the chicken tractor's function as he'd given his uncle. "You said you didn't want your garden disturbed," he concluded, "so this is the first step in building a second garden. The chickens will do all the work preparing the ground."

He saw wary approval on her face but she said nothing. Instead, per his direction, she stationed herself at one end of the structure as he put himself at the other. Carefully they flipped over the entire thing so it rested on its casters.

Jacob decided that he would stop rising to the bait if Rebecca needled him in any way. Instead, he set himself to be pleasant. It was the least he could do to honor Caleb's decision to gift him the farm.

"Will this be too heavy for you?" he asked, once the chicken tractor was standing on its casters.

Rebecca tried to lift it. "*Ja.* Does it have to be carried or can we drag it?"

"Drag it," he replied. He found some rope and fastened it to the handles on either side of the structure. "Let's try it."

Moving slowly, they pulled the tractor out of the barn and toward the chicken coop.

"How will you get the chickens into this?" she asked, panting slightly, as the tractor lay alongside the fence to the chicken yard.

"I'm going to cut a small hole in the fence and put the mouth of the tractor against it," he replied.

"I have a better idea. Put the mouth of the tractor against the opening to the yard, and I'll entice them in."

"How?"

"I'll be right back." Rebecca trotted off, then returned in a few moments with a jar of something. "Okay, let's move it to the gate."

They tugged the tractor toward the gate and opened the sliding hatch. Rebecca began sprinkling oatmeal from the jar through the chicken wire, then called, "Here, chick, chick, chick!"

With amusement, Jacob watched as all twenty birds came squawking and flapping for the meal. The transfer took less than thirty seconds, and he dropped the hatch to close them in.

He outright laughed. "That was *gut*! Caleb said you knew livestock like the back of your hand. I'm impressed."

She laughed back, and Jacob caught his breath.

He'd seen her smile before, but this was literally the first time he'd seen her laugh. As before, it transformed her face.

"Danke," she said, watching the chickens pecking at the oatmeal in the pen. "I love working with animals. Even before I moved here, milking cows and feeding horses was one of my favorite things to do. And chickens? They're just fun." She paused a moment. "I think I'll take the opportunity to give their coop a thorough cleaning while everyone's out."

"But first, could you give me a hand moving this into location?"

Together they tugged at the rolling tractor. The hens clucked in alarm as they were nudged along under the screened shelter. Good thing they didn't have far to go.

"I just want to pull it alongside the garden," grunted Jacob. "*Ja*, this is *gut*." He adjusted the structure near the garden fence.

He stood back with Rebecca and watched as the chickens immediately started pecking at the grass, scratching and otherwise searching for insects and other edibles. "I could use your help with preparing the ground for the new garden," he said, then ventured on. "And also, I wouldn't mind knowing how it is your parents let you travel to Montana to work for Caleb. It's a long way for a single woman to travel alone."

Her face shuttered. "That question came out of the blue."

"Maybe so, but I'm curious."

She turned away and plucked a tall stem of grass, shredding it. "Let's just say my parents—especially my *mamm*—did me wrong. I was very angry. I think they knew they'd better let me cool off if they wanted to salvage the relationship. Traveling here was my way of cooling off. And that," she added fiercely, "is all I'm going to say about it. My private life is none of your business, Jacob. I'm here to help on the farm, that's all."

"It doesn't *have* to be."

"What do you mean?" She eyed him suspiciously.

"I mean, if we're going to be working together, we should be on friendlier terms." He smiled. "Friends tell each other things."

"We're not friends, Jacob." Her voice was flat. "We're coworkers. You're my boss, I'm your employee. Let's keep this professional, shall we?" She dropped the grass stem. "Now tell me what you plan to do with this new garden space."

Jacob didn't know whether to be amused or irritated by Rebecca's attitude. One thing was certain: she was a tough nut to crack.

He'd never met anyone with such a fierce streak of independence. What could have caused it? He found himself intrigued by her…possibly as more than just a coworker.

Chapter Four

Over the next few days, Rebecca found herself working alongside Jacob while doing chores on and around the farm.

"How much milk are you getting per day?" he asked, standing over her as she milked one of the three Jersey cows Caleb owned.

"Right now, about six gallons." She kept her usual efficient pace while they chatted. "About two gallons from each cow. I don't milk in the evenings. I just let the calves stay on their mothers all day and separate them at night, then milk in the morning. That gives the calves plenty of milk, and we have more than enough for our needs. Six gallons a day is plenty to make cheese and butter."

He nodded. "*Gut* idea."

"I thought it was common practice," she countered. "Unless you're in the business of selling milk, why would you want so much?"

"That's what I often asked my *bruder*. He insisted cows must be milked twice a day."

"Well, of course they do, if the calves are removed."

"*Ja*, but your method makes more sense. Let the cows raise their own calves. It seems easier."

She was surprised at his support. "You said you worked for your *bruder* for a long time?"

"Ja." She saw a scowl creep onto his face. "He was… set in his ways."

"Aren't we all?" She finished milking the cow, tucked a covering over the bucket and moved it away from the milking stall. "Here, why don't you release Bossy into the pasture? I'll be done with the next cow in a few minutes."

And so her chores went. Jacob seemed interested in every aspect of her job. He didn't criticize or show her a different way to do something; he merely watched and asked about her techniques.

Rebecca found herself trying to prove to Jacob that she was worth keeping as an employee. Every chore she performed was done perfectly. The barn had never been so clean, the butter had never been so pure, the chicken coop had never been so scrubbed.

One afternoon, she sat on a crate in the vegetable garden, weeding. She liked weeding. For her, it was an excuse to be still and enjoy the sounds of nature. It was, in fact, her favorite prayer time.

So when Jacob came inside the fenced garden area and began walking around the beds, examining them closely, she was just the slightest bit annoyed.

She watched him with narrow eyes. Would he find fault with her gardening techniques? Criticize her choice of plants to grow? It was a big garden and he started at the opposite side, peering at the plants, and worked his way over to her location.

Subtly, Rebecca looked him over. He was a fine specimen of a man, she had to admit, with the wiry muscles of a farmer and the fiery eyes of someone passionate about his work.

He finally made his way toward the bed where she was weeding. "Well?" she asked. "Does the garden meet with your approval?"

"*Ja* sure," he replied mildly. "It's impressive how much you grow. You also have a nice bed of celery, I see." He gave her a cheeky grin.

She felt her cheeks grow hot. "Caleb likes it in his stews," she said shortly.

Celery had a reputation among church members as an indicator of courtship, since the vegetable often adorned wedding tables. Growing celery was often a silent announcement of intent for the bride's family.

Jacob didn't seem inclined to dwell on the celery. "But you're always weeding," he continued. "I'm thinking of ways to make the garden less work."

"I *like* weeding," she replied.

"I don't," he responded with a slight twinkle in his eye. "Maybe that's why I'm looking for ways to make things easier."

"That seems to be one of your interests," she noted. "Me, it's just part of a day's work. Why are you so focused on making things easier?"

To her surprise, he drew up another crate and sat down on the opposite side of the raised bed, then started pulling at weeds. "My father almost worked himself to death," he said quietly. "Seeing how much effort he put into farming made me reluctant to take it up myself. But then I came across this system called permaculture, and while it takes some time to establish, in the long run it requires less effort because it works in cooperation with the land rather than fighting against it."

"How do you keep weeds from growing?" she inquired, waving a yanked-up plant in the air. "It's just a given for a garden."

"*Ja und nein.* Heavy mulch will discourage weeds, especially if it's packed in, after the vegetables get a *gut* start. Mulch won't eliminate all weeds, but enough that the plant isn't outcompeted."

"But I have mulch." Rebecca pointed to a layer of straw on the garden beds.

"*Ja*, but not enough. If you packed it in thicker, it would retain more water, as well as prevent more weeds from growing."

"That's what you said earlier," she observed musingly. "More work at first, then easier in the long run."

"*Ja*, exactly." He seemed pleased.

"Caleb has wheat straw from last year's crop," she offered. "He keeps it for bedding for the animals, but there's plenty. I suppose it could be used on the garden beds."

"Really?" He jumped up from the crate. "Show me!"

Rebecca also rose, then dusted off her hands on her apron. She was amused by Jacob's boyish enthusiasm for something as mundane as mulch.

He followed her into the barn, to where several unused stalls were heaped with straw. "This is perfect!" he exclaimed. "Can you help me mulch the garden beds?"

"*Ja* sure." Rebecca seized a wheeled cart and handed Jacob a hayfork. They packed the cart with straw and wheeled it to the garden.

"Mulch is one of the mainstays of permaculture," he gushed, expertly packing a two-inch layer of the vegetation around the garden plants. "My guess is you'll be able to cut watering down to once a week once the whole garden is mulched."

It took several hours for the entire garden to be finished. When the last bed was mulched, Rebecca stood up, arched her aching back and surveyed her domain. "It *does* look better," she admitted.

"And the weeds should stay away," he agreed. "*Danke*, Rebecca. I think you'll be pleased with the results."

"Weeding was always my prayer time," she teased. "Now I'll have to find another mindless chore for that purpose."

He grinned and locked eyes with her, and suddenly her breath was caught. In a teasing mood, Jacob didn't seem like the nemesis she had made him out to be.

Confused, she turned away and picked up her hayfork. "Well, I need to get the calves into their pen for the night."

"And we need to return the chickens to their coop." He also picked up his hayfork and placed it inside the wheeled cart.

A whole day. She had been working with him a whole day without a cross word. Rebecca wasn't sure she could keep up the wall she had constructed to keep him at arm's length.

Together, they completed the evening chores.

"I wonder what Caleb is making for dinner tonight?" mused Rebecca as they pulled the chicken tractor back to the yard.

"It's so funny how he discovered he enjoyed cooking after Aunt Naomi passed away," Jacob reflected.

"He told me it was a way to fight off loneliness," she said. "But he doesn't like doing dishes, and that's something I've never minded doing, so we're a *gut* team. Usually we trade off. Whoever cooks doesn't have to clean up."

"Then what will *I* do?"

"Maybe you should learn to cook." Rebecca couldn't quite keep the tartness from her voice. "After all, Caleb will be leaving in a month, ain't so?"

"Maybe. I offered to build him a *daadi haus*. He's thinking it over."

"Really?" Rebecca turned to him, eyes wide. "That would be *wunnerschee*!" She smiled.

He shot her a look. "You really are fond of him, aren't you?"

"*Ja*, of course. I said that earlier. He's become like a *grossdaddi* to me. We've always gotten along."

"Is that the only reason you're fond of him?" With one final tug, Jacob positioned the chicken tractor in front of the coop and slid open the trapdoor to allow the chickens to return to their yard.

She drew her eyebrows together. "What do you mean?"

"I mean, you've already admitted you hoped Caleb would leave the farm to you. Is that the only reason you're fond of him?"

Rebecca drew herself upright and glared at him. "Of all the ridiculous accusations," she spluttered furiously. "Why do you find it so impossible to believe that I've grown to love him? Why are you so suspicious of me?" She whirled around and ran—literally ran—back to her cabin.

After slamming the door behind her, she burst into tears. How could he? How could he possibly think her affection for Caleb was based on anything but genuine love for the older man?

Did Jacob honestly think she had worked all these years for Caleb solely on the hope of personal gain? Had she ever given him that impression? Had Caleb ever hinted at it?

No. It seemed he just pulled that assumption out of thin air, and Rebecca found herself deeply offended that he would judge her in such a harsh light.

Both of her grandfathers had passed away while she was a *youngie*. She remembered them well and with great fondness. In her heart, Caleb had taken their place—not just in teaching her life skills, but in offering her refuge in her time of need, as well as sympathy and advice when she needed it.

And now to have Jacob taint their relationship with his suspicions was unbearable.

Tomorrow was a church Sunday. Rebecca was looking forward to the reprieve from doing any work with such a stubborn, skeptical new boss.

She sniffled and wiped her face with a handkerchief, allowing herself a grim smile. Caleb would wonder why she wasn't at dinner. Hopefully, Jacob would admit that what he'd said was wrong. She could only imagine the kind of tongue-lashing Caleb would give him.

Jacob watched Rebecca fly down the path toward her cabin. He heard the distinct slam of the door, and felt immediately ashamed.

Whatever his private thoughts about Rebecca's motives, he shouldn't have voiced them out loud. For a moment, he thought about going straight to her cabin to apologize, but he had a feeling she would be less than open to forgiveness at the moment.

Slowly, he headed for the main house, knowing Caleb would want an explanation for Rebecca's absence at dinner.

Inside the kitchen, the older man was stirring something in a pot. He looked up when Jacob entered. "I'm trying a new recipe," he said happily, gesturing toward an open cookbook on the table. "It's a lentil dish with rice and some spices. Rebecca loves lentils. I have a feeling she's going to like it."

"Ah… Rebecca won't be joining us," Jacob said. He hung his hat on the hook by the door.

Caleb stopped stirring. "She won't be joining us? Why not?"

The moment for truth had arrived. "Because I said something that made her mad," he admitted.

"Jacob, you didn't." Caleb tapped the spoon on the edge of the pot, then laid it on a plate next to the stove. He turned to face his nephew. "What did you say?"

"I…" Jacob sighed. "Well, I basically accused her of

working for you all these years in hopes that you would leave her the farm."

If he expected fury from the older man, he was surprised when, instead, Caleb gave him a look of the most profound disappointment. In a way, it was worse. "You have no tact, Jacob," he said bluntly.

"*Ja*, I know." Jacob dropped onto a kitchen chair and scrubbed his hands over his face. "Though I was too candid, it came from the truth. Rebecca is very disappointed at not being your heir, having worked for you all these years."

"I thought she might." Caleb picked up the spoon and continued stirring.

Jacob stared at his great-uncle for a moment in silence, then asked, "Let me ask you a question, Uncle Caleb. Why *did* you leave the farm to me? Without any children of your own, you were free to will it to anyone. Why not Rebecca? Why reach all the way across the country to me?"

"Because a man needs a farm to support a family." Caleb gave Jacob a sad smile. "When Naomi passed away, it was too hard to stay on the same property where we spent so many happy years. That's why I sold our farm and moved here. But I kept in touch with everyone back home in Millersburg, and your *daed* told me of your frustration working for your *bruder* with no land of your own. I had it in my head for a long time that I'd give this farm to you."

"Words can't even begin to express my gratitude," acknowledged Jacob. "You know that better than anyone. That said, I have to admit I understand Rebecca's anger at the situation."

Caleb turned away from him for a moment, took some bowls out of a cabinet and began ladling food into them. From the oven, he removed some crusty garlic bread. "She has her own place to live and her own job duties. She can just keep on doing what she's been doing for me for the last five years, and be a huge asset to you."

"I don't think she would want to." Jacob rose from his chair to gather cutlery and napkins, and hastily set the table. "At this point I think she's more interested in just getting away from me."

"That would be a shame." Caleb smiled with catlike satisfaction. "However, there is a way to convince her to stay, and make her happy about the inheritance situation as well."

"How?"

"Get married."

"Caleb!" Jacob whirled around and stared at his uncle. "You can't be serious!"

"Why not? It would solve the inheritance issue for everyone."

"And make two people miserable for the rest of their lives! Rebecca and I get along like oil and water. You know that."

"Well, you can't blame an old man for trying."

Jacob wasn't sure he liked the twinkle in his uncle's eyes. He had never been the subject of matchmaking before, and found himself rather uncomfortable.

"Nein," he replied firmly. "I wouldn't do that to Rebecca, even if she was willing. Marriage is a lifelong commitment. It would be a disaster to unite two people who fight like cats and dogs."

Caleb sat down and paused for a silent blessing on the food, then bit into a piece of garlic bread. "Then you may just have to put up with her as a thorn in your side, unless or until she decides to move on. But really, Jacob, is it so bad having her around? You've been here almost a week. You've seen how hard she works."

"*Ja*, I have. I can see why you're fond of her, too. But a marriage between us would never work."

In fact, just the idea of being pushed into marriage with Rebecca filled him with unease. He thought of all the happy marriages he knew—Caleb and Naomi, his parents, his brothers, his sisters… They all had spouses they could lean on during good times and bad.

But himself? *Nein.* He had no one…and realized he would rather remain alone than marry someone who rubbed him the wrong way.

"So why *haven't* you gotten married?" Caleb pressed. "You're older than most men when they decide to plant some celery."

"Most of it was because I wasn't in a position to support a family yet," Jacob admitted. "This dish is excellent, by the way." Jacob hoped to distract Caleb from his love life.

"*Danke.* Now, with your own farm, that's no longer an issue. You'll start meeting everyone at church tomorrow. Perhaps a young lady will catch your eye."

"Perhaps," Jacob answered, in between bites of the delicious lentils.

"Was there anyone back in Ohio you might want to encourage to move out here?"

"*Nein.* Most of the women my age are married by now.

I suppose that was part of my frustration—knowing I couldn't get married without having a farm of my own. As a middle son, I should have learned a different vocation, but I've always wanted to be a farmer."

"And now here's your chance. So what is this permaculture you keep talking about, anyway?"

With great enthusiasm, Jacob launched into an abbreviated lecture on agriculture, explaining the basic principles of the alternative method. "It won't undo what you've accomplished here," he assured him. "But it approaches farming differently. In just the few days I've been here, already I can tell how different Montana is than Ohio, both in climate and in soil. In some ways, it's a perfect setup to see how effective the system will work with a different environment. That's also why I'm pleased to see your beehives. Bees are an integral part of the system."

"Well, Rebecca is the beekeeper," Caleb reminded him. "If you want to keep the bees, you'll have to keep her."

"How hard can it be to become a beekeeper?"

"Oh, Jacob." Caleb gave him a half smile. "Those are arrogant words. She's been working for a long time to overcome some of the pests bees are subject to, as well as learning how best to keep the bees from dying off in the winter. Don't think you can just step in and learn everything in a summer. Beekeeping, I've realized, is an intricate art."

"Well, if she decides to move on, I guess I'll have to learn, then, won't I?"

"*Ja.* Don't try to chase her off, though."

"I won't, Uncle Caleb." Jacob stared at his nearly empty bowl of food. "To be honest, I'm ashamed of what I said that chased her off. Whatever my private suspicions, I shouldn't have said them out loud."

"*Ja*, you're right. But we're human and we make mistakes. It seemed you were getting along earlier today, mulching the garden together."

"*Ja*, we were. It kind of surprised me, but we were. She certainly does work hard." He thought about how the sunlight lit up her *kapp* and illuminated her dark eyes. She might have a prickly personality, and she might have a touchy disposition, but she sure wasn't hard to look at.

"Uncle Caleb, let me ask you something. Why isn't Rebecca married? At her age, that's a little unusual. Do you know?"

"*Ja*, I do." The old man wiped his mouth with a napkin. "But I won't say. She'll tell you when she's ready."

Jacob wondered if there was some sort of scandal or tragedy in her past. Those were the usual explanations for an unmarried person within the Amish church.

"Meanwhile," Caleb continued, "there's enough lentils and garlic bread for one more person. Do you want to run it over to Rebecca's? I know she doesn't keep a lot of food in the cabin since we normally eat our meals together."

"Nein." Jacob gave his uncle a grim smile. "In her state of mind, she's likely to toss it back in my face."

"That bad, eh?"

"Spitting mad," Jacob admitted.

His uncle chuckled to himself.

"One thing is certain," Jacob said as he rose from the

table. "I'm doing the dishes tonight. Not only did Rebecca tell me as much, but I feel guilty for annoying her, so it's the least I can do."

Caleb chuckled. "Then it's all yours, my boy. Consider it your penance."

While Jacob gathered the bowls and cutlery and started washing them, he kept an eye on Rebecca's cabin, which was visible from the kitchen window. The building was dark and quiet. Part of him wanted to go knock on the door and apologize, but instinct told him she wasn't in a state of mind to be receptive to his remorse.

He thought about Caleb's half-jesting suggestion that he and Rebecca get married to solve the inheritance issue.

Ha. What a ludicrous idea. It would never work.

Right?

Chapter Five

After a restless night's sleep, Rebecca rose early. Being hungry didn't help her mood. She had chores to do before church, and hoped she wouldn't happen across Jacob while doing them. He was absolutely the last person she wanted to see at the moment. After milking the cows, she even brought the milk back to her cabin to strain and chill rather than risk running into Jacob in the main house.

But seeing him was unavoidable. It was a church Sunday. He would undoubtedly be riding in the same buggy as Caleb and her.

She dressed for church, brushed and coiled up her hair, repinned her *kapp* and walked over to the main house, prepared to do battle.

Caleb was alone in the kitchen, packing a hamper for the after-church lunch. Rebecca's conscience pricked. That was normally her job.

"Guder mariye," she said. "I'm sorry, Caleb, I should have packed the basket."

"Guder mariye," he replied, eyeing her. "Are you all right?"

She wondered how much Jacob had told him last night. "Fine," she answered in a neutral tone. She rummaged around the kitchen for items to put in the hamper.

"But hungry, *ja*?"

"Ja," she admitted.

"You missed a wonderful dish. It was a new recipe, too—lentils and rice with that new berbere spice I bought some time ago. Your portion is in the icebox."

"*Danke*. Maybe I'll have it for dinner."

It wasn't the most creative lunch basket they had ever packed—normally she spent time on Saturday making some dishes for Sunday's potluck meal—but between her and Caleb they managed to pull together enough to fill it to the brim. By the time it was ready, Rebecca heard the sound of a horse and buggy pulling up to the house.

"I'll sit in back," she told Caleb.

He nodded as if he was aware of her reluctance to face Jacob. *"Ja gut"* was all he said.

When she emerged from the kitchen, she refused to meet Jacob's eyes, and muttered an uncharitable *"Guder mariye"* to his greeting. She climbed into the back seat of the buggy and Caleb handed up the basket of food. Once the older man had settled himself in the front seat, Jacob clucked to the horse and they headed down the road.

Somehow it felt sacrilegious to be on her way to church while filled with anger and sulkiness, but she couldn't see her way past the emotions. She glared at the back of Jacob's straw hat as he expertly guided the horse, following Caleb's directions toward the Stoltzfus house, where the service was being held.

She missed the old days of camaraderie and easy companionship with Caleb. In just one week, their relationship of five years had been altered by the presence of an arrogant, know-it-all intruder…

She caught herself from going further down that path. "Forgive me, *Gott*," she whispered, and tried instead to focus on her surroundings.

It was a pretty May morning. They passed some families walking to the farm owned by Amos and June Stoltzfus where the service was being held. Many others came in buggies drawn by horses with shiny coats. She nodded and exchanged subdued waves with other families.

Once Jacob pulled the buggy to a halt in the area near the barn, she vaulted out and reached for the basket. "I'll go put the food on the table," she said to Caleb, abandoning him and Jacob to unhitch the horse on their own.

She joined the throng of women placing baskets and hampers of food on the long line of boards set up on sawhorses used as makeshift tables. She nodded and smiled to various women, but said very little. Socializing happened after the church service, not before. Then she headed into the newly cleaned barn where the church service was being held, and gravitated toward the women's side.

She scanned the familiar faces quickly. When she saw her friend Eva Hostetler sitting demurely with her nine-month-old son on her lap, she sat next to her, hoping her stomach wouldn't growl too loudly during the service. Eva nodded a greeting and smiled. The pretty matron had her daughter sitting on the other side, and her older son was no doubt sitting with her husband across the aisle on the men's side.

The Hostetlers were a solid, respectable family, well-liked and active in the community. More crucially, neither Eva nor her husband, Daniel, was the type to gossip. Rebecca couldn't imagine better people to help her in her quest to find another living arrangement if and when the time came to leave Caleb's farm.

The service proceeded like most church services: hymns, an introductory sermon, prayers, scripture readings, the main sermon given by the bishop, testimonies, then finally closing prayers.

Afterward, the bishop made some announcements, and welcomed Jacob as the newest member of the church as well as the community of Pierce, mentioning his relationship to Caleb and that he would be inheriting the farm. Rebecca kept her eyes on the floor of the barn. Did she imagine it, or was there a stifled collective gasp from some people at the news Jacob would inherit? She didn't look up, so she didn't know if she was the recipient of any startled glances.

Jacob stood up briefly to acknowledge the bishop's welcome, then sat back down on the bench beside Caleb.

When it was time to file outdoors for the potluck lunch, Rebecca made sure to linger with Eva. "How's this little man doing?" she inquired, reaching for the baby. She bounced little Eli Joseph up and down in her arms. "He's getting so big!"

"*Ja*, he's an armful." Eva chuckled as her baby son

reached for his mother again. "He's at the age where he only wants his *mamm* or *daed* to hold him."

"Someday I'll have one of my own," Rebecca said, startled that she'd said such a thing.

Eva shot her a look but said nothing as they began unpacking baskets and laying out the food for lunch.

Clusters of men gathered around Jacob, shaking his hand and introducing themselves, while Caleb stood nearby with a benevolent smile on his face. Rebecca jerked her gaze away. Of course the church members would welcome him. They didn't know he was an arrogant, know-it-all intruder.

Soon everyone stood in line to fill their plates with food and break off into groups of family and friends. Rebecca loaded her plate with fried chicken, macaroni salad, corn chutney and some cold biscuits to fill her empty stomach, then walked over to sit with the Hostetlers.

"How's the bee business?" asked Eva's pleasant husband, Daniel.

"Gut." Rebecca smiled. "I split eight hives earlier this week and it seems they've all settled in well. If none of them fail, that will give me a total of fifty-four hives. Hopefully, there will be enough honey to harvest in the fall from the split hives. Usually I give them a year to build up their reserves before taking any excess to sell."

"You amaze me." Eva shook her head. "I've never known a beekeeper before."

"They're fascinating creatures." Rebecca took a bite of macaroni salad. "I've learned so much in the last five years."

Conversation soon turned to other matters that affected them and the entire community. Rebecca waited for an opportunity to broach the subject that was hanging heavily on her shoulders.

"Do either of you know anyone interested in hiring a farm hand?" she finally asked.

"Why?" Daniel sipped from his glass of lemonade. "Do you know someone looking for work?"

"Well, I might be." She kept her eyes on her plate to avoid the inevitable reaction from both husband and wife. She added, "With Jacob taking over most of the heavy chores on Caleb's farm, I might be needing a new job soon."

There was a moment's startled silence. "Trouble?" asked Eva softly.

"Ja," Rebecca admitted, but said nothing more. After the bishop's announcement, the Hostetlers could draw their own conclusions, but she knew they wouldn't probe.

After another few moments of silence, Daniel nodded. "I'll keep my ear to the ground and let you know of anything. Is it urgent?"

"*Nein, nein*, not at all. I'm just…exploring the possibilities, that's all."

At that moment, Eva reached out and touched Rebecca gently on the hand. "Caleb's farm isn't too far away from ours," she remarked. "If you ever want to come over for a cup of tea, you're always welcome."

"Ja, danke." Rebecca blinked back the sudden moisture in her eyes. Eva's offer to unburden her cares was clear—and welcome. It wouldn't hurt to discuss her

problems with the warmhearted woman. "I might take you up on that."

Eva's invitation was more appreciated than she realized. It occurred to Rebecca that she had been stewing in her own misery without any outside perspective. Eva would be the perfect person to listen to her concerns and possibly offer some advice. Rebecca made a mental note to have some tea with her during the upcoming week.

But Eva took the bull by the horns. "Mondays are my least busy days," she said firmly. "Why don't you come over tomorrow around two o'clock? I've been wanting to try a new cookie recipe anyway, and you can be my test subject."

"*Danke!* I'd like that," Rebecca said.

"He doesn't seem like a bad sort," remarked Daniel, glancing in Jacob's direction.

"He's not," Rebecca reassured him hastily. "And he's so *gut* with Caleb. We've just had some…disagreements."

"What about the beehives?" inquired Eva. "If you move to another farm, what will happen to the bees?"

"*Gut* question." Rebecca furrowed her forehead. "It has me worried," she admitted.

"Could they stay where they are until winter?" suggested Daniel. "I can't imagine so many hives would be easy to move when they're active at this time of year."

"*Ja*, perhaps. But it would also mean going back onto Caleb's farm to tend them." Rebecca sighed. "It's complicated, ain't so?"

"Are things so bad that you feel it's better to leave?" asked Eva gently.

Rebecca felt her eyes prickle. "It seems that way sometimes."

"We'll do what we can to help," Daniel assured her.

"I would be grateful if you didn't mention this to anyone," said Rebecca. She motioned toward Bishop Beiler, who was approaching Jacob. "Right now, I'd rather keep it private."

"You have our word," Eva promised her.

Despite his suspicions that Rebecca had spent five years cozying up to Caleb solely to inherit the farm, Jacob regretted saying it so bluntly to Rebecca. Now, as he watched her avoid him all day, he knew he had only himself to blame.

Sitting next to Caleb on the men's side during the church service, he could hardly focus on the hymns or the sermon. Rebecca sat on the women's side, looking demure and pretty in her gray dress and white apron. He tried not to stare, but found himself watching her from the corner of his eye. From that angle, she seemed devout and full of piety, and hardly like someone scamming his uncle for his money and land. Was he wrong?

At the conclusion of the service, the bishop—a tall, lanky man with a wispy beard and an air of quiet authority—introduced him as Caleb's grand-nephew. The church members started filing out of the barn, and soon Jacob found himself surrounded by men shaking his hand and welcoming him to the community.

"Guder nammidaag!" said one. "I'm Adam Chupp."

"I'm Benjamin Troyer."

"Aaron Lapp."

"Thomas Kemp."

He smiled and returned greetings, but knew it would take a while to sort out names and faces.

He stood in a cluster of men, Caleb at his side, and listened to talk of community projects—building a house for a newly arrived family, adding a second floor for a couple with an expanding family and constructing a *daadi haus* for an older couple wanting to retire. He received invitations to participate, and agreed to them all. He knew the best way to be accepted in his new church home was to be as helpful and active as possible. Besides, he liked carpentry.

When the food was spread out on the makeshift tables and people started lining up to fill their plates, he noticed Rebecca hovering near the same woman she'd sat with at church. She didn't look at him, and he got the distinct impression she was doing all she could to avoid him.

"Hungry?" inquired Caleb, steering him toward the food line.

"Ja," he admitted. "I like the people I've met so far. This seems like a nice community."

"*Ach*, it is. It seems you'll hardly be at home, with all the invitations you received," his uncle teased.

"I could hardly refuse, now, could I?" Jacob smiled at his mentor. "And I enjoy swinging a hammer as much as the next man."

They filled their plates and found seating near Adam Chupp.

"Jacob, this is my wife, Ruth," Adam introduced.

"Guder nammidaag," Jacob replied, shaking hands

with the pretty woman, who held a year-old baby in her arms.

"Guder nammidaag," she replied. "How do you like it in Montana so far?"

Conversation over lunch was cordial as he learned a little about his new acquaintances. Toward the end of the meal, the bishop strolled over.

"We haven't been properly introduced," he said. "I'm Samuel Beiler. Welcome to the church."

Jacob rose and shook hands. "*Danke.* Everyone's been so friendly. I'm glad to be here."

"I'd like a chance to meet with you in private," said the bishop. "Just to get an idea of your background and experience. When is a convenient time?"

"Anytime." Jacob had been half expecting the request. Such meetings were not unusual. "My hours are my own. Would today work?"

"*Ja* sure. In fact, you can come with us back to the house in our buggy, if you like."

"Danke." Jacob reseated himself as the bishop sauntered away. "Seems like a *gut* man," he remarked to the group.

"Oh, he is." Adam bit into a biscuit. "He's one of the best bishops I've ever known. We're fortunate to have him steering this motley crew of a church."

"We have people settling here from many different states," added Ruth, letting her baby son gum a cookie. "Bishop Beiler is tasked with smoothing over issues with a wide variety of people. He's very skilled at it."

"I look forward to getting to know him better," Jacob replied, but a hint of doubt entered his mind. Had the bishop also assumed that Rebecca would be Caleb's heir? He suspected he would soon find out.

Finally, the potluck was winding down. Women started gathering plates and dishes, and repacking hampers. Men broke down the tables and benches, and packed them into wagons. Jacob made himself as useful as possible. When the barn and yard were clean and some buggies were already heading out, he made his way over toward the bishop.

"*Ach*, Jacob, have you met my wife, Lois?" inquired Bishop Beiler.

"Nein. Guder nammidaag," said Jacob, shaking hands with a short plump woman with twinkling eyes. "Can I help you up?" He assisted her into the buggy.

"Danke," she replied.

He climbed into the back as the bishop seated himself next to his wife, picked up the reins and clucked to the horse.

"What a lovely day it is," said Lois, looking around her with alert eyes. "We originally came from Pennsylvania, so this part of the country took some getting used to. Now I can't imagine living anywhere else."

"Ruth Chupp mentioned the church members in this settlement come from all over," he replied over the sound of the clopping hooves. "How did it get started?"

"Things were getting too crowded back east," said the bishop, his hands firmly on the reins. "Several church leaders started scouting for land in the west. A huge ranch came up for sale outside the town of Pierce here in Montana. It wasn't selling because it was so big, so the price was reasonable for the amount of property.

The church bought it, and has been dividing out parcels ever since. It's exciting to be part of a new settlement. There are still many sections available for incoming families at far more affordable prices than comparable property in Pennsylvania or Ohio or Indiana."

"From a leadership standpoint, it must be a challenge," remarked Jacob. "Everyone who settles here has a slightly different church background, *ja*?"

"Ja," the church leader replied. "But we've had no troubles. Everyone understands those differences. What we're doing, then, is forging our own path on the settlement. *Gott ist gut.*"

A few minutes later, the bishop drew the buggy up to a smallish home which looked like a made-over barn, with a large garden space up front and barn in back. Virginia creeper twined around the porch rails, and colorful flowers edged the walkway.

"Lois will get you a glass of lemonade while I unhitch," Bishop Beiler said.

Jacob trailed after the bishop's wife, listening as she chattered about the beauties of the countryside. Within a few minutes, the bishop entered the house. "Come into my office," he invited.

His office was spare but comfortable. A beautiful calico cat slept in a basket on the desk.

"This is Thomasina. She's my favorite pet." The bishop tickled the animal under her chin and a loud purr filled the room. "Now, tell me how you're settling in at Caleb's."

Jacob outlined how his week had gone, and decided to be honest about his issues with Rebecca. "She's been surly and uncooperative since I arrived," he admitted. "Caleb says it's very much outside her typical behavior. My suspicion is that she'd hoped to be Caleb's heir, and resents my very presence because Caleb selected me instead."

"I confess it took a lot of people here by surprise."

Jacob blinked in astonishment. "Did *everyone* expect Rebecca to inherit the farm?"

"*Ja*, probably." The bishop stroked his beard with an air of distraction. "Did you know in advance Caleb had chosen you?"

"*Nein.* It took me completely by surprise. I can't even begin to express how grateful I am, too. Uncle Caleb told me he chose me as his heir so that I'd have the opportunity to provide for a wife and children."

"At the expense of Rebecca," murmured the church leader.

A thread of irritation went through Jacob at the implied blame, but he kept his expression neutral. "It's not my doing, I assure you."

"Perhaps not, but I find myself concerned nonetheless." The bishop folded his hands on the desk and looked at Jacob seriously. "It's my job to watch out for the welfare of the community. If there's going to be issues between you and Rebecca, then I'd like to do what I can to help. Above all, I don't want things getting out of hand and it causing the community to divide into factions."

"Factions?" Jacob drew his eyebrows together in a frown. "What do you mean?"

"Rebecca is well-liked here. So is Caleb. I expect you will be, too. But if there's conflict between you and Rebecca, it might escalate to the point where people are taking sides. That's why I want to know in advance if there's anything I should help with."

"I can assure you, Bishop, nothing that serious has arisen. Yet."

The bishop's eyebrows rose. "Please let me know if it *does* turn serious."

"*Ja*, I will." Jacob fought the urge to get out of there. This was his church leader. He couldn't flee just because the conversation made him uncomfortable.

Fortunately, Bishop Beiler seemed to sense the same thing and turned to less awkward subjects.

However, by the time Jacob emerged in the afternoon sunshine, he wasn't sure if he should be relieved or disturbed by the rumors swirling about his conflict with Rebecca. There were few secrets in the church community.

It was to be expected, among the Amish. But he'd never been talked about in this way before, back in Ohio.

Was there a way to settle this "disagreement" between him and Rebecca? It was something to ponder as he walked back to the farm.

Chapter Six

Crouched over the milking bucket the next morning, Rebecca was startled when Jacob entered the barn, issued her a polite *"Guder mariye"* and started cleaning one of the horse stalls. Stranger still, he issued a stream of chitchat entirely out of keeping with her prior experience with him.

Finished milking the cow, she stood up to release the animal from the milking pen. "Are you feeling all right?" she asked him sourly.

"*Ja*, I'm feeling fine," he replied. "Why do you ask?"

"Because you're talking up a storm. That's not like you."

He gave her a sunny smile. "Just trying to be friendly."

"Well, stop it. It's odd."

His eyebrows rose. Did she detect a glint of humor in his eyes? "Odd?"

"*Ja.* Yesterday I don't believe you spoke two words to me. The day before, you insulted me. And suddenly this morning you're trying to be friendly?" She crossed her arms and glared at him.

He chuckled, though it sounded slightly forced. "Let's just say I've decided to turn over a new leaf. Although I *do* owe you an apology for what I said Saturday afternoon. That was uncalled for, and I'm sorry."

Mollified, she turned to pick up the milk pails. "*Ja*, well, forget about it." She turned her back on him and marched toward the main house.

"*Guder mariye*, Rebecca." Caleb turned from where he was frying some sausages in a pan as she came in through the outside kitchen door.

"Guder mariye." She heaved the buckets onto the kitchen counter and prepared to strain the milk. "Jacob is acting rather funny this morning."

"How so?"

"He was chattering up a storm and acting friendlier than usual." She fitted a clean cloth into a colander over a jar. "He even said he's turning over a new leaf. Frankly, I don't trust him."

"But what if he is?" Caleb said. "Turning over a new leaf, that is?"

"Then I'd wonder why." She saw concern in the older man's eyes and sighed, somewhat ashamed of herself. "I'm sorry, Caleb. This has nothing to do with you."

"*Ach*, but it does." Caleb turned the sausages in the frying pan. "It's my hope that you and Jacob will be able to establish the same productive working relationship as you and I have. After I've left for Ohio, there should be 'peace within thy walls, and prosperity within thy palaces.'"

Despite herself, Rebecca smiled. That was one of Caleb's favorite psalms.

"Besides," he continued, "if he's being friendly, let him be friendly, and see where it leads."

"See where it *leads*?" Rebecca turned a sharp eye on her mentor. She wasn't sure she liked the sound of that. "What do you mean?"

"Nichts," he muttered, and to Rebecca's concern he blushed.

Now she was well and truly alarmed. Was Caleb pushing her toward Jacob as a *hutband*?

Before she could ponder this further, the man in question bustled into the kitchen and sniffed the air. "Smells *gut*," he observed. He went to the kitchen sink to wash his hands.

Rebecca remained silent. She didn't trust Jacob's sudden friendliness or Caleb's cagey hints. What was going on?

She didn't trust matchmaking. What she hadn't told Jacob was why her betrothed, Jeremiah, had left her at the altar. He told her he simply wasn't attracted to her.

At the time, Rebecca had tried hard to mold herself into what she thought Jeremiah wanted in a wife. She worked hard, never complained and built up his ego. It was, to some extent, an artificial facade, and after the sting of humiliation at his desertion faded, she realized she might well have been as unhappy as Leah had she gone through with the marriage.

Coming to Montana meant a fresh start. Never again would she be anything but her real self. She was stubborn, yes. And opinionated. She wasn't the prettiest woman around. But she would far rather remain single than be yoked with a man who couldn't appreciate her for the way *Gott* made her.

Now here she was, five years later, happier than she'd ever thought possible. Oh, sure, she received gently scolding letters from her mother periodically, wondering why she hadn't settled down yet. But Rebecca wasn't about to be pushed or bullied into marriage until *Gott* sent her the right man. There weren't a lot of single men here in Pierce, so Rebecca simply accepted that she was single and was determined to enjoy it.

After what happened during her younger years, anything even vaguely hinting at matchmaking was awful to her. Like a young calf being trained with a lead rope, being pushed toward a man made her want to dig in her heels and resist at all costs.

Rebecca shuddered. Why must elders focus on getting all the young people married off? Why couldn't they leave well enough alone?

Even if Jacob had turned over a new leaf with his sudden geniality, she vowed to respond to it on a surface level…no matter how much Caleb might make hints.

"I'm visiting with Eva Hostetler today," she announced to everyone over breakfast. "She invited me to tea."

"Who's Eva Hostetler?" asked Jacob, as he cut into a sausage on his plate.

"A very nice woman who lives about a mile away. She's one of my favorite people out here."

"*Ja*, the Hostetlers are *gut*," agreed Caleb. He smiled benevolently at Rebecca. "It's been a while since you've had tea with her. I hope you have a *gut* time."

After breakfast, she cleaned up, washed the dishes, then weeded the garden until it was time to leave for Eva's. Rebecca smoothed her apron and checked her *kapp*, then set off down the gravel road.

The May afternoon was sparkling and warm. Despite her current conflicts with Jacob and even Caleb, Rebecca let the peace of the day flow over her. The air smelled fresh and clean, birds sang from groves of conifers along the road and she waved to the occasional church member driving by in a buggy. Very few *Englischers* ever ventured into the Amish settlement near Pierce, and she enjoyed the feeling of security the isolated area offered.

Approaching the two-story house with a fenced yard, she heard Eva yell, "Come in!" in response to Rebecca's knock.

Eva's house was in a state of pleasant chaos, with the older children helping make cookies and the youngest baby crawling around the kitchen floor.

As often happened when visiting Eva, Rebecca felt a pang of longing. The Hostetlers were a content family. Eva and Daniel were devoted to each other, and the children were happy and well-behaved. Though Rebecca and Eva were about the same age, Eva seemed so much further along in life.

"Have a cookie," offered the young matron. She filled a teakettle and placed it on the propane stove, then lit the flame. "These little ones are probably eating them as fast as they're making them."

"What kind are they?" Rebecca reached for a treat. "You said you were trying a new recipe?"

"*Ja*, they're jam-filled oatmeal cookies. Kind of messy

to make, so I multiplied the recipe to get it all done at once." Eva gestured toward one of the children using a round can to cut shapes. "See? I roll the dough thin, the *kinner* cut them out, then we put a dollop of jam in the center, sandwich it with another cutout and bake them."

"Delicious." The cookies were hearty and not too sweet. "You'll have to give me the recipe."

"*Ja* sure. Meanwhile, you can pour yourself some tea and tell me what's going on at Caleb's."

Knowing the children were too young to understand their conversation, Rebecca decided to be honest with her friend about the situation on the farm. She explained her dark hope of inheritance. "Then Caleb pulls Jacob out of his back pocket and suddenly I'm not even in the picture anymore. Caleb thinks things should be able to continue on as before—that I'll stay on and continue working the farm as I've always done. But Jacob's made it clear he won't need my help."

"Does Caleb know Jacob doesn't want you around?"

"*Ja* sure. He's worried, I know. Then, Saturday night, Jacob hurled an accusation at me that made me furious. He knows how fond I am of Caleb. He also knows I'd hoped he would leave the farm to me. So he asked me if my fondness for Caleb was real, or if I was faking my feelings for Caleb in the hope that he would leave me the farm."

Eva made a sour face. "Ouch."

"*Ja.* That did it for me. There's something about Jacob that just rubs me the wrong way. We can barely be in each other's company without arguing. Until this morning." She sipped her tea.

"What happened this morning?"

"He was friendly and chatty and even said he was trying to turn over a new leaf. I flat out told him it was odd."

Eva chuckled as she went to pull two sheets of cookies from the oven, and slid two more trays in.

"Then, Caleb..." Rebecca gave a small groan. "Then he said something even more worrisome when I mentioned Jacob's behavior. He said, 'If he's being friendly, let him be friendly, and see where it leads.' Does that sound like matchmaking to you?"

To Rebecca's surprise, Eva clapped a hand over her mouth to cover her laughing.

Rebecca eyed her sourly. "What's so funny?"

"*Ja* sure, it *does* sound like matchmaking. I just find it funny how a man old enough to be your grandfather is doing that."

"Well, I won't have it."

Eva sat down and picked up the baby, who was trying to crawl up her legs. She cuddled him on her lap. "So why *haven't* you gotten married?"

"Because I just haven't met the right man yet." That wasn't quite truthful. She hadn't even been looking. Rebecca reached for another cookie. "And let me assure you, Jacob is *not* the right man. It irks me that if I continue to live on Caleb's farm, I'm going to have to deal with him on a daily basis. That's why I'm going to start searching out a new place to live." She sighed. "And taking the bees with me could be...complicated."

"*Ja...*" agreed Eva.

Before she could say anything further, there was a

knock at the door. Eva hoisted her baby son into her arms and rose to go answer the door.

"*Guder nammidaag*, Eva." It was a teenager's voice. "Is Rebecca Hilty here?"

Rebecca rose and saw the visitor was Jonathan King, the youngest son of Ephraim and Mary King, who lived not far away.

"*Guder nammidaag*, Jonathan," she said, walking up to the door.

"My *daed* sent me to find you," the boy said, panting a bit. "I went to your place first, and Caleb said you were here. We have a swarm of bees in our yard and *Daed* wondered if you could take care of them."

"*Ja* sure!" She loved hiving a swarm of bees. "But I'll have to go home and get some equipment, then hitch up the buggy. How long have they been there?"

"Maybe half an hour."

"There's a chance they'll move before I get there, but I'll do my best. *Danke*, Jonathan. Tell your *daed* I'll be there as soon as I can."

"Bitte." The boy turned and ran off.

"Sorry to cut our visit short." Rebecca leaned over to kiss Eva on the cheek. "Thanks for listening—and for the cookies."

"I'm always here if you need me. And I'll write down the cookie recipe for you later on."

"Ja gut. Faeriwell."

Jacob heaped some wheat straw into a wheelbarrow and trundled it out to the garden space he wanted to expand. His mind, however, was not on his work.

He was thinking about Rebecca, and that bothered him. Why should such a troublesome, stubborn, opinionated woman be on his mind? It didn't help that Caleb seemed to have matchmaking on *his* mind.

And yet… Jacob pitched some straw on the ground and spread it with a hayfork. The more he thought about it, the less against the idea he became. And that worried him.

His romantic past was almost nonexistent. Sure, there had been a few pretty girls he'd been interested in courting in his younger days, but without an adequate way of supporting a family, he knew better than to pursue marriage. The women he had fancied were all married now, with *kinner* of their own.

Now he had a farm and could court anyone he liked. The problem was, as he learned at church on Sunday, there weren't a lot of eligible women his age in the Amish community here. Except… Rebecca.

Certainly she wasn't as pretty as some of the women back home. He wondered if her stubbornness and independence was what kept her from marrying earlier. But really, was that kind of personality so bad? He wanted someone with a mind of her own, someone with whom he could engage in spirited conversation.

As if *Gott* heard his thoughts, he saw Rebecca walking quickly across the barnyard. She went straight into the part of the barn where the buggy was kept.

What happened to her afternoon with Eva Hostetler? Curious, Jacob pushed the empty wheelbarrow into the barn and found her hitching up one of the horses to the buggy. "Something wrong?" he inquired.

"There's a swarm of bees at the Kings' farm," she told him. Wiping a bead of sweat from her forehead, she continued hitching up the horse. "I'm going to go hive them."

"How do you hive a swarm?"

"I don't have time to explain right now. I have to get over there as soon as I can, and I still have to get a spare hive and my bee veil from the cabin."

"Can I go with you?" Jacob was curious how she worked with the bees, and hiving a swarm seemed like a prime opportunity.

Rebecca paused and looked surprised. "*Ja* sure," she said after a moment. "I have a spare bee suit you can wear. Caleb sometimes came with me to hive a swarm."

"I can finish hitching up the buggy," he offered. "That way you can get whatever equipment you need."

"Danke." There was a note of uncertainty in her voice, but she didn't waste any time. She hurried out of the barn.

Jacob finished hitching up the horse, vaulted into the seat and directed the animal to Rebecca's cabin. She was pulling a sturdy cardboard box about two feet square from a shed. Then she added a folded-up white sheet, a large net bag, a bee brush, pruning shears, a bottle of some sort of liquid and a step stool. Piled on top were white coveralls with attached veils, and long gloves.

"Got everything you need?" he asked.

"*Ja.* Don't get down, I'll have everything loaded in a moment." She hauled her equipment to the back of the buggy and heaved it in, then climbed into the seat. "Let's go."

"You'll have to direct me." Jacob started the horse down the driveway toward the road.

"The Kings' farm is about a mile way," she said. "You'll need to turn left at the first intersection."

"So you call it 'hiving a swarm,'" he said. "What does that mean, exactly?"

"Bees will often swarm in spring and summer," she replied. "It's normal. Hives will swarm for two basic reasons. Either they're overcrowded and just need to split, or there was something wrong with the hive—lack of resources, or the queen was ill, or the hives were disturbed too often, or disease. I don't know whose bees these are. I don't think they're mine. I just split a bunch of hives the day you arrived. And I've been monitoring my bees for disease and everyone seems healthy. This might be a swarm from someone else's hives."

"If that's the case, are you obliged to return them?"

He was surprised when she gave a chuckle. "*Nein.* First of all, I would have no idea whose bees swarmed. And second, in the beekeeping world, there's a finders-keepers rule of thumb. If you're fortunate enough to come across a swarm, it's yours."

"So how do you take a swarm home?"

"It's easier than you think. But while I can get the bees into the box easily enough—assuming the swarm isn't too high up in a tree or something—I won't bring them home right away. That's because the scout bees—the individual bees who are actively looking for a new nest location—are out and won't return until just before dusk. My hope is to hive the swarm, including the queen, and then leave the box at the Kings' farm and return this evening at dusk to pick it up."

"You certainly know a lot about bees," he remarked. "It doesn't sound like something I could step into at a moment's notice."

"*Nein*, it's not. I've been keeping bees for five years now, and still consider myself an amateur."

"How did you get involved with bees to begin with?"

"It was Caleb." Her face softened, as it often did when mentioning her mentor. "I never gave much thought to bees until he suggested getting some shortly after I arrived in Pierce. I took a class and got the equipment and my first nucs, and I've been hooked ever since."

Jacob didn't know what a *nuc* was, but it didn't matter. It was clear she was passionate about the insects. And if he planned to take over the care of the hives when Rebecca left, he had better learn all he could.

"The Kings' farm is there." Rebecca pointed. "You see that driveway near the huge pine tree? Turn onto it."

Within a few minutes, Jacob pulled the horse to a halt in front of a sturdy older farmhouse. The whole King family was standing on or near the porch. Ephraim, the patriarch, descended the porch steps.

"*Guder nammidaag*, Rebecca. Jacob," he greeted. "Rebecca, *danke* for coming. I don't quite know what to do with these bees."

"Don't worry. I'll take care of them." Rebecca climbed down from the buggy seat. "Are they still in the same location?"

"*Ja.*" Ephraim brushed a hand in front of his face as a bee darted by. "*Komm*, I'll show you."

Wondering if they should don their protective clothing first, Jacob climbed down from the buggy.

Jonathan, the family's youngest son, stepped forward. "I'll hitch the horse over there in the shade," he offered.

"Danke," said Jacob gratefully. He hurried after Rebecca and Ephraim.

As he approached, he saw a cluster of bees grouped on a low branch of a shrub near the barn. Ephraim had stopped a respectable distance away.

"Perfect location," Rebecca said to Ephraim as Jacob walked up. "It won't take any time to get the main group in the box, but I won't want to take the box home until this evening, after the scout bees return."

"Ja gut," the older man said. "Just do whatever you need to."

To Jacob, it seemed Ephraim was nervous about the bees being so close to the barn, and he couldn't blame him. The enormous gathering of bees was an intimidating sight. The air was thick with random insects flying around, though it was clear the vast majority were grouped on the branch. The sound of humming was almost unnerving. Maybe it was Jacob's imagination, but he could almost sense an electric vibration in the air, a feeling of pent-up activity.

"What's the first step?" he inquired as Rebecca and Ephraim turned to walk back to the buggy.

"The first step is to get suited up," she replied. "Normally I don't wear a full suit, but in this instance I don't want to risk getting a bee up my skirts." She grinned, and he was momentarily taken in by the sparkle of mischief in her eyes. "I think Caleb's suit will fit you."

"Why are beekeeper suits white?" he asked, as she handed him the zip-up coverall with the veiled headpiece hanging down.

"It's kind of a neutral color for bees," she replied as she removed her shoes and fitted her feet into the legs with elasticized cuffs of her suit. She stuffed her skirt inside, zipped the coverall up to her neck and slipped her shoes back on. "Bees tend to see large creatures in dark colors as predators, like a bear, so wearing dark colors will almost guarantee you'll get stung. Colors are one of the main factors that will either drive bees into action, or prevent them from doing so."

"Right. White it is." Jacob found himself slightly nervous now that he would be so close to the bees for the first time.

"Zip it all the way up," Rebecca advised, when Jacob left a small gap at his neck. "That's right. Now watch how I put on the veil, because you don't want to leave an opening, especially in an important place like the neck."

She pulled the veiled headpiece over her head, and he watched as she first zipped it fully around the neckpiece of the suit, then fastened the dangling Velcro straps secure across every junction.

Awkwardly, he tried to follow her efficient movements, but zippering the veil was more complicated than he anticipated.

"Here, let me help." Rebecca stepped forward, her features slightly obscured behind the veil. She zipped his veil to the suit top, then fastened the straps. "There. Unless you press your face to the netting of the veil, the bees won't be able to sting. That was the first time

I got stung," she added in an amused voice. "I was so fascinated by what I was seeing in a colony that I had my face pressed right against the veil. A bee stung me on my cheek." She chuckled at the memory.

It was an odd time to feel a flash of interest in Rebecca, attired as they both were in the bulky suits. But he suddenly realized how self-assured and confident she was in the face of thousands of stinging insects. He found that an attractive quality.

"One last thing." She handed him a pair of gloves, with elasticized sleeves that went almost up to his elbows. "Now let's go catch that swarm."

Chapter Seven

It was the first time Rebecca had ever had an audience when working with bees. Most people, without the protection of a bee suit and veil, kept a respectful distance when she worked with the insects.

But now she had a double audience—the King family, who stayed on the porch, and Jacob, who was close at hand.

"First thing to know," she told Jacob, "is to keep your voice low—no shouting or loud talking. And keep your movements slow and calm, too. Bees are remarkably quick to pick up agitation or anger or other strong emotions."

"How likely are we to get stung?" Jacob asked with a trace of nervousness in his voice.

"Not likely at all," she said with some surprise. Was he concerned about that? "Have you been stung before?"

"*Nein.* How bad is it?"

"Not bad. I mean, it's a bit painful, but not as bad as you'd think. Even when I work directly with hives, I seldom get stung."

"I saw you working the hives wearing just a veil."

"*Ja*, sometimes it's easier. Here, despite their appearance, bees in a swarm are remarkably calm because they have nothing to defend—no hive, no honey, no brood. All they have to do is make sure their queen is safe, and since she's smack in the middle of the swarm, she can't get much safer than that."

"What's the sheet for?" he asked as she shook it out.

"I put this on the ground below the box. This evening when I collect the swarm, I wrap the box with the sheet to keep the bees inside."

She picked up the bee brush, the white sheet and the cardboard box, and approached the cluster of bees with Jacob at her side.

"Now listen carefully," she told him. "This swarm couldn't be in a better location. They're low to the ground, so I don't have to climb a ladder or anything. But I can't have you making any noise or exclamations at what I'm going to do. Is that clear?"

"*Ja* sure," he replied. "But what are you going to do?"

"It's very simple. I'm going to put the open box right beneath the swarm, then shake the branch sharply. That will knock the majority of the swarm straight into the box, including the queen. It sounds crazy, but most of the bees will stay in the box because they don't want to leave their queen."

"I'll stay quiet," he promised.

She nodded, remembering how she'd marveled when she'd first watched a beekeeper in Pierce hive a swarm. The *Englischer* had been her beekeeping mentor during her first year, and she had learned a tremendous amount. "Here, you can hold this," she said, and gave him the bee brush.

The hum of the swarm as she drew near never failed to fascinate her. They were so vibrant and full of promise. Keeping her movements smooth, she spread the white sheet on the ground beneath the bush. In the center of the sheet, directly under the cluster, she placed the box with its flaps out. Then, grasping the branch of the bush where the bees were gathered, she gave it a single sharp shake.

With textbook perfection, the majority of the swarm simply dropped into the box with a dull thud. She heard Jacob's faint gasp.

The hum of the swarm increased in agitation at the sudden change in location, but true to form, most of the bees stayed inside the box, a living, writhing mass of insects. A few hundred stayed clinging to the tree, and a few hundred more fretted about the box, crawling up the flaps or buzzing low over the interior. Hundreds more swirled in the air in confusion.

With the majority of the cluster in the box, she shook the branch a few more times to dislodge any stragglers. "That should have gotten the queen," she said to Jacob in satisfaction.

"How do you keep them in the box?" he asked quietly.

"Most will stay there, because hopefully that's where the queen is," she replied. Working with slow movements, she tucked the flaps in to secure the box. "See these holes?" She pointed to the upper sides of the box, where triangular sections had been cut out. "The bees will follow the queen's pheromone—her particular scent—into the box." She stood up. "That's all we can do at the moment. It will take a few hours for everyone to settle down, and for the scout bees to return and find the queen."

"Scout bees?"

"*Ja*, the individual bees whose job it is to find a new home. They're roaming around right now. Meanwhile I have to go home and get a new hive set up for them."

"Amazing," he murmured. Through the veil she saw wonder on his face.

She chuckled to herself, remembering her own first experiences with bees that rapidly morphed into an obsession. *"Ja,"* she agreed. "Honeybees are one of *Gott*'s most remarkable creations. Watch out, Jacob, or you might get bitten by the same beekeeping bug I did."

"It might be too late," he admitted.

"Let me have the bee brush," she said, and took the brush from him. "Now turn around. I want to make sure you have no stray bees clinging to your suit." She brushed a few clinging insects off the garment, then had him return the favor, especially on her back.

"They can't sting through the fabric?" he asked, brushing an insect off her shoulder.

"Not really, unless the fabric is stretched tight across the skin, such as at knees or elbows. But most of the time people have the suits over their regular clothes anyway, which adds an extra layer of protection. That's about all we can do for the time being," she added. "If you want to get the buggy ready, I'll go talk to the Kings." She walked away from the buzzing box of bees toward the King family, stripping off her gloves as she did so. She unzipped her veil and let it dangle down her back.

"That's it," she told Ephraim King with a smile. "I suggest no one go near the box right now. There's going to be a lot of activity around it for the next few hours. I'll be back this evening."

"*Vielen dank*, Rebecca." Ephraim mopped his forehead with a handkerchief. "That was something to see."

Rebecca didn't contradict him or explain why a swarm was so much more docile than a hive. Since a swarm was one of the dramatic wonders of nature, it would be rude to dismiss his awe.

"I'm grateful for the new colony," she told him. "I'll bring a quart of honey for you this evening when I pick up the box."

"Danke!" Ephraim grinned. "We'd like that."

Amid the chorus of appreciation from the family, she walked toward the buggy, where she found Jacob struggling with the zipper to his veil, unable to remove it from the neck of the suit.

"How does this thing work?" he muttered in frustration.

"Here, let me help. It takes a while to get the hang of these things." Stepping close, she reached toward the back of the neck, where the zipper started, and got the headpiece unfastened.

It was the second time she had been so physically close to Jacob, and—dressed as they were in the white beekeeper suit over their everyday clothes—she still found the experience surprisingly intimate.

As soon as she was finished, she stepped back and let him raise the veil and let it drop backward. *"Danke."*

"Bitte."

His blue eyes seemed unusually dark as he caught her gaze and held it for a few moments. She turned away and started pulling at Velcro tabs on her own suit. She realized she wasn't ready for a truce with Jacob. It seemed easier somehow—and safer—to cling to resentment rather than reach an armistice.

Silently, she peeled off the suit, stepping out of her shoes to remove the legs, then bundled the garment into the back of the buggy. She didn't look at Jacob as he, too, awkwardly divested himself of the coverall. She climbed into the buggy seat as he untied the horse. In a few minutes, they were trotting toward home.

"How often does that happen?" Jacob asked. "Catching a swarm like that?"

She breathed a silent prayer of relief. It seemed Jacob hadn't been as shaken by that moment of closeness as she had. What was wrong with her?

"It depends on the time of year," she replied, glad her voice sounded normal. She took a deep breath, then continued. "Last year I caught four swarms in one month, and nothing the rest of the year. Bees almost always swarm in a short window, right about now. It happens when a hive is overcrowded. That's why I work on splitting hives in the spring, to try and avoid swarming."

"And you'll be able to settle this swarm into a hive without a problem?"

"*Ja.* Almost certainly. Bees just want a roomy place to live. That's what I'll give them."

"Can I watch as you set up the new hive and settle them in?"

"*Ja* sure." She was faintly surprised. It seemed Jacob had, indeed, been bitten by the beekeeping bug she had teased him about earlier.

She wondered if she minded. Except for the *Englisch* mentor in town who had helped her get started, she hadn't found anyone in her church community who shared her enthusiasm for bees. Caleb was supportive, but not really involved. For five years, her project had largely been a solo endeavor.

Now here was Jacob, acting all interested. A small part of her wondered uneasily if there was an ulterior motive to his interest.

But she couldn't worry about it now. She tried to be happy he was intrigued by the insects, and leave it at that.

This was Jacob's first experience with honeybees, and he found himself just as fascinated as Rebecca warned him he'd be.

"I'll help you get a new hive set up, if you want," he offered as he pulled the buggy to a stop in front of the barn. He was eager to see how she did it.

"Ja gut," she replied, a hint of uncertainty in her voice. "I keep some empty hive boxes in the barn."

He climbed down from the buggy and unhitched the horse. He gave the animal a brief brushing, then released it to the pasture with an affectionate pat on the flank.

He went back into the barn to find Rebecca pulling various things from a dark corner. "Do you know where the cart is?" she asked, referring to the sturdy wheeled cart Caleb often used for barn chores.

"*Ja.* I'll go get it." He fetched it, pulling it into the barn.

"This is a platform base," she said, handing him a stout, short-legged stand. "It's what the hive will be set on. I don't like setting hives directly on the ground. A platform helps keep pests like mice or insects from trying to get inside. Caleb made me a bunch of these when I first got started."

"Did he make the rest of this, too?" he asked as she handed him various other components of a hive—a brood chamber, bottom board, cover, frames—and a garden rake. He duly piled everything into the cart.

"Nein," she replied, brushing dust off her apron. She had a smudge of dirt on her cheek, which he found adorable. "I bought the equipment premade. Caleb offered to make it, but since he had no previous experience making hives, and they tend to be standard sizes, I felt it was safer to buy them."

He pushed the cart out of the barn as Rebecca led the way to the bee yard. "Wait, do we need the bee suits?" he asked, suddenly remembering.

"Nein." She didn't break stride. "We're not working directly with the bees, and the bees in all the other hives will just ignore us since we're not a threat."

"Ja gut."

He had never really spent any time in the bee yard except for Rebecca's brief tour when he first arrived, but now he looked around more attentively. The yard was simply a clearing on the edge of some trees. Dozens of hives were in a loose circle, and the log from a fallen tree was at one end. Some of the hives had brood boxes painted various pastel colors—pink and blue and green and yellow—while the rest of the hives were white. Some had other boxes piled higher, which he remembered she called "supers."

"I think I'll put the new hive there." Rebecca pointed to a spot.

"Why are some of the hives painted different colors?" he asked as he pushed the cart where she indicated.

"To help the bees identify which one is theirs," she replied. "Bees are very attuned to color, and also to cues from their surroundings. If I were to take, say, that pink hive and move it to the other side of the bee yard, it would completely confuse the bees because I've changed not just the location, but all the cues they pick up from the surroundings to pinpoint which hive is theirs. If a hive must be moved, it should either be moved just a couple feet away, or *very* far away so they're essentially starting over."

"Which is what you're doing with the swarm, *ja*?"

"Ja." She glanced at him, and he saw approval on her face that he understood. "Exactly so. If the swarm accepts the new hive—and I'm confident they will—it means they'll become used to their new home and learn it by the landmarks around them, including color and placement of other hives."

She pulled the rake out of the cart and vigorously leveled a section of ground, then set the platform base on the raked area, positioning it so it didn't wobble. He watched as she assembled the hive, which took just a few minutes. He noticed she set aside several of the frames.

"You don't want to put these in with the others?" he asked, pointing to the frames.

"*Nein*, I'm going to paint them with a sugar-water solution first," she replied. "That will help encourage the new bees to stay in the hive. I'm also going to put a feeder of sugar water in the hive as well, but I'll do that tomorrow. There." She stepped back and brushed off her hands, a look of satisfaction on her face. "This will be humming with bees by tomorrow morning."

"It's already humming." Now that the assembly process was finished, quiet descended on the bee yard and the indistinct hum of the other hives was audible.

"*Ja*, it is." Rebecca's voice was quiet and held a thread of joy as she absently leaned the rake against the log. He glanced at her and saw she was looking around the bee yard, her gaze lingering on other hives. "Sometimes I will just come here and sit on that log and let the peace of watching the bees at work envelop me. Sometimes I think I'm closer to *Gott* while sitting on that log than I am in church."

It was an unusual statement and a peek into the raw emotion of her soul. He said nothing, just watched the expressions on her face.

She was a complex woman, and a prickly one. But at moments like this, when he saw the passion with which she regarded her cultivated insects, he wondered if she could ever cultivate a similar passion for human companionship. She was alone, yet not alone. She had her bees. It seemed they were all she needed.

He wasn't sure whether to be relieved or alarmed by that thought.

"Can you show me around the hives and tell me about them?" he asked quietly after a moment. He was reluctant for the interlude to end.

"*Ja* sure." She started walking around the bee yard.

He trailed after her, half listening as she explained a brief history of each hive, when she added supers, how she checked the health of the queen and other particulars. "I'm selecting hives that show a resistance to varroa mites," she told him.

"How do you do that?" He found himself interested despite his ignorance of the science of beekeeping.

"It's not too hard." She pointed to a hive painted pale green. "I take the colonies with the strongest natural resistance and split them to make two strong colonies. At first, I lost quite a few hives to the mites—over half. But year by year, the number of losses drops. Last year I only lost a quarter of the hives." A smile crept across her face and her gaze took on a faraway look. "There's a lot of satisfaction in breeding healthy bees. It's an addicting pastime."

"And this swarm you just captured? How will they fare?"

"I won't know until a year from now, next spring. Before winter, I'll do everything I can to help the bees survive the cold weather. I certainly won't harvest any honey from most of the hives, especially this new one. But you see that?" She pointed beyond the hives, toward the surrounding fields.

"See what?" Jacob wondered if she had another hive outside the bee yard.

"The flowers." She started walking toward a ring

of plants growing in a broad swath around the entire bee yard. She touched some greenery with her toe. "A few years ago I planted a whole bunch of nectar-heavy wildflowers in a circle around the bee yard. I made sure to only use species native to this area, so the bees will have a lot of foraging right nearby."

"Amazing," he murmured. Rebecca's activities with the bees, he realized, were part of the kinds of projects he hoped to accomplish as part of his permaculture goals on the farm. He would be wise to learn as much from her as possible so he could maintain the hives after she left.

"I'd like to see how you pick up the swarm this evening, and put the bees in this new hive," he offered.

"*Ja* sure." That note of uncertainty was back in her voice. He suspected she harbored suspicions about his motives. "I think the bees will be settled in a couple hours. We can pick them up then. But I won't hive them until tomorrow morning, early."

He nodded. "What time?"

"Just after sunrise, before the day gets warm."

"How do you put that box of bees into the hive?"

She smiled. "You'll just have to wait and see, won't you?"

He smiled back. "*Ja.* I will."

For a moment he caught her eyes and his heartbeat quickened. There was something mischievous about her expression, and he realized that she was quite a captivating woman. Not classically pretty, but she had a strong and intelligent face.

"Well..." He stepped back and looked around the bee yard. "I'm going to work on some other things for the rest of the afternoon. Let me know when you want me to hitch up the horse and go get that swarm."

"I will, *danke*." He noticed she seemed skittish all of a sudden.

It discomfited him to think they might be heading for a truce. His goal on Caleb's farm was to run it according to his own guidelines. It was something he had desperately wanted since he was a teenager, and *Gott* had providentially provided him with the opportunity through Caleb's generosity.

Keeping Rebecca on as a farm hand wasn't part of those plans, no matter how much Caleb might urge to the contrary.

But there was a difference between need and want. He may not *need* Rebecca to stay...but maybe he *wanted* her to.

Chapter Eight

After cooking dinner, Rebecca left Caleb to wash the dishes. With some relief, she prepared to fetch the box of bees from the Kings' farm.

She felt relief, because while she was cooking dinner, she was fielding Caleb's curious questions. First, he had asked about the swarm, which led to more questions about how Jacob had reacted to the beekeeping activities, which in turn had segued into how she felt about Jacob.

"He seems to know what he's doing on the farm, don't you think?" Caleb asked. He sat at the kitchen table, a cup of coffee at his elbow, in a familiar pose.

"He seems to know what he wants to do, *ja*," she replied, chopping broccoli. "He has some sort of vision about this place, the whole permaculture thing."

"I'm still not quite clear what it means or how it differs from regular farming," Caleb admitted. "But whatever it is, he likes having the bees here. He's been talking about them more and more."

"I suppose that's why he wanted to see how to hive

a swarm, then." Rebecca tossed the broccoli with a bit of oil and some spices, and spread the vegetables on a pan to roast them. "I guess he's thinking about keeping some of his own hives if I leave and go to work somewhere else." She slid the pan into the oven.

"I'm trying to convince him you're too valuable to let go." Caleb stroked his beard, something he did when he was thoughtful or troubled. "Maybe the bees are the answer. Does he know they're all yours, including all the hive equipment? Does he know that if you move away, the bees go with you?"

"I don't know." Rebecca began chopping some chicken. "But if he finds himself that interested in beekeeping, nothing's preventing him from starting his own hives. There's an *Englisch* beekeeper in town that might be willing to act as his mentor."

"What about you?" inquired Caleb. "If he wanted to start beekeeping, could *you* act as his mentor?"

She tamped down a sigh. "This is all theoretical, Caleb. I don't know whether I'm staying or leaving, I don't know if Jacob knows the bees belong to me and I don't know if he's truly interested in getting bees or not."

"Are you two getting along better?"

"I've promised myself not to lose my temper in his presence, if that's what you're asking." She smiled at him.

"He's a handsome fellow, don't you think?"

Her smile widened at the blatant question. "What does that have to do with bees?"

"Nothing. Just pointing out the obvious."

"Caleb, I hope you're not inclined toward matchmaking. You know how I feel about that."

"*Ja* sure, but Jacob isn't like the man you say your *mamm* matched you with, is he?"

"*Nein*, nothing like. But that doesn't mean I'm looking to be courted, either." She kept her voice firm. "These things can't be pushed, Caleb."

Rebecca didn't know whether to be amused or irritated by the older man's persistence. He seemed to think that just because she and Jacob were being forced into each other's presence on various projects, it would inevitably lead to some sort of romantic spark. She wasn't quite sure how else to quell that notion except with bluntness.

Caleb gave an exaggerated sigh. "I suppose I'm at an age where I understand why your *mamm* was interested in matchmaking. I look upon you as a granddaughter, Rebecca, and I worry about your future."

"I look upon you as a *grossdaddi*, Caleb." Rebecca kept her voice gentle, but she once again questioned why, if the older man was so concerned about her future, he would leave the farm to a great-nephew instead. But it was still a question she did not feel comfortable asking. It smacked too much of greed and avarice to imply she was more deserving of the property than Jacob.

The man in question came into the house right then, through the outside kitchen door. She quailed for a moment, hoping he hadn't overheard any of the previous conversation.

He washed his hands and talked cheerfully about how the swarm would be transferred from the box to the hive, while Rebecca looked at him with a narrow gaze.

She had avoided seeing Jacob as anything more than an impediment since his arrival, but now she tried to see him through the eyes of a disinterested stranger.

Caleb was right—Jacob *was* handsome in a conventional sort of way. His hair was curly, his eyes had laugh lines at the corners and he had the lean, wiry look of a farmer. He definitely ticked many boxes of what she found attractive in a man.

But she just couldn't overlook his role in what might, ultimately, result in her leaving the farm for another position. This whole situation wasn't Jacob's fault, but it made little difference in her resentment.

However, she kept to her decision to at least be pleasant. She didn't want to disrupt the warm friendship she had with Caleb, despite his decision to favor Jacob over her.

At the conclusion of dinner, she rose and said to Jacob, "Let's leave for the Kings' place in about half an hour. It will be close to dusk by the time we get there."

"Ja gut," he replied.

Half an hour later, she climbed into the buggy seat while Jacob finished lighting the oil lanterns to hang at either side of the vehicle. She tucked a quart of honey on the seat next to her as a thank-you gift to the Kings. Jacob climbed in next to her, took the reins and directed the horse out of the courtyard by the barn and onto the road.

"Where will the bees stay tonight?" he asked.

"Probably just on my porch," she replied. "I intend to take them out to the bee yard even before sunrise."

When the buggy drew up to the Kings' house, Ephraim

and his family spilled out to greet them. They seemed eager to witness the next step in the swarm wrangling.

"It won't be as dramatic as earlier today," Rebecca warned the patriarch with a smile. "All I'm doing is wrapping the box in the sheet, then putting the net bag over everything. But here, this is for you." She handed him the honey.

"Danke!" Ephraim took the jar with a smile and handed it to his wife. "Your honey is some of the best!" He paused a moment and said wistfully, "I wish we had bees here on the farm, for pollination if nothing else."

"Nothing prevents you from getting some," said Rebecca.

"Except I don't want to be a beekeeper. I just like having them around." Ephraim gave her a lopsided grin. "Does that make sense?"

"*Ja*, oddly it does."

Jacob interrupted. "Do we need to suit up again?"

Rebecca suspected he was a bit nervous about the idea of handling the bees without protection, even during a time they were unlikely to cause problems. "*Ja* sure," she replied.

They spent a few minutes dressing themselves in the coveralls and veils, and then—once again watched by the King family from the porch—approached the box on the ground. She carried a large mesh bag. The white sheet looked bright in the gloom, with the box sitting in the middle of it.

Rebecca peered around the cardboard box. "Looks like everyone's settled in," she said with satisfaction. "Catching a swarm isn't always this easy. Here, grab that corner of the sheet and help me tuck things in."

With Jacob's assistance, she tied the sheet around the box, then lifted the whole package into the large mesh bag Jacob held open. She tied off the end of the bag, and together they gently carried it to the buggy and laid it in the back seat. "That will keep any stray bees from escaping," she said, unzipping her veil.

"That was certainly easier than I thought it would be," Jacob replied, pulling off his gloves and climbing into the buggy seat.

Rebecca thanked the Kings once more, then joined him in the buggy.

"*Ja*, it's not that complicated to catch a swarm, especially when they were so low to the ground." From behind, a subdued humming could be heard. To Rebecca, it was a comforting sound. "Assuming this swarm takes to the new hive, this now makes fifty-five hives on the farm," she mused.

"Having this many hives is such an asset," Jacob replied, starting the horse down the darkened road. "It makes the farm so much more productive."

"*Ja*, it does. I've had people ask me to put hives on their farms as well. Up until now, I hadn't really thought about doing that, but maybe it's something I should consider." It occurred to her that, if she was required to leave Caleb's farm, then scattering her hives among many different locations might be a better strategy than trying to find somewhere else she could set up a bee yard with all the hives in the same spot.

"This could be a full-time job rather than a part-time one," remarked Jacob.

To Rebecca, the casual statement seemed to have

more sinister overtones. Was it a veiled reminder that her days on Caleb's farm were numbered?

"Ja," she replied warily. She made a mental note to follow up with this morning's conversation with Eva Hostetler. And perhaps she should put out the word about settling hives on other people's farms sooner rather than later. "Working the bees full-time might be *gut* insurance for the future."

She was aware of Jacob glancing sharply at her, but he said nothing. The rest of the drive home was conducted in silence.

All night long, Jacob thought about bees. He even dreamed about them—a dream in which he was attired in a bee suit and working alongside Rebecca as they maintained the colonies.

He woke up early, because he wanted to see how she transferred the swarm to the hive. He smiled to himself. Had he been bitten by the beekeeping bug, as Rebecca had warned?

The morning dew was thick upon the grass as he quietly let himself out of the house through the kitchen door, the bee suit over his arm. Jacob sniffed the air. He liked it here in Montana. Without the heavy blanket of humidity he was used to in Ohio, the air seemed fresher somehow. Birds twittered in the trees. A flash of pure blue caught his eye, a bird Caleb said was the mountain bluebird. The eastern horizon was bright but the sun had not yet risen.

He saw Rebecca step outside her cabin. She hadn't noticed him as she bent to examine the mesh bag holding the box of bees, and he took a moment to admire her trim figure. She had an air of dignity and efficiency about her that he admired. Whatever the future held for her, he was certain she would do very well.

"Guder mariye," he called quietly.

She jerked upright. "Gracious, you startled me! *Guder mariye.* You're up early."

"You said you wanted to move the swarm into the hive before sunrise. I want to see how you do it. You're right about being bitten by the beekeeping bug," he added. "I find myself eager to learn more about them."

She chuckled. "I warned you."

"*Ja.* Now what can I do to help? Should I carry the bag?"

"*Ja, bitte.* However, I recommend suiting up before we move them."

They spent a few minutes pulling on the coveralls, adjusting the straps and zipping the veils into place. Jacob was pleased he was becoming more efficient with donning the complicated suit.

"Ready?" he asked her.

"*Ja*, ready." She picked up a small bottle and followed as he carefully hoisted the mesh bag containing the sheet-wrapped box.

The sun was just peeking over the eastern horizon when they stopped at the hive in the bee yard. Jacob saw very little activity from the bees at this early hour.

"It's because the temperature is too cool," explained Rebecca when he asked her about it. "Bees really don't become active until the air temperature is about fifty-five degrees. It's about fifty degrees right now, but it will warm up quickly when the sun is fully up."

He carefully lowered the bag with the box to the ground as Rebecca lifted off the lid to the empty hive box, then removed all the frames.

"These are the ones I painted with sugar water." She indicated two of the frames. "I'll put those in the middle. Meanwhile, let's get these girls in the hive. I'm sure they're tired of being in the box."

He helped remove the mesh bag, then untied the sheet surrounding the box.

"Lay the sheet flat on the ground," directed Rebecca. "That way any stray bees that get outside the box and caught in the sheet will be able to get to the hive."

She opened the flaps to the box, and Jacob peered inside at the seething mass of insects, buzzing and crawling around, but mostly clustered at the bottom. He was glad to be wearing a bee suit. "How do you transfer them to the hive box?"

"First, I'm going to put a few drops of lemongrass oil in the hive box," she said, lifting the small plastic bottle with a flip cap she had been carrying. "It resembles a pheromone, which the scout bees use to guide the swarm to their new home." She dabbed the oil around the hive entrance as well as inside the hive, then capped the bottle and slipped it into a pocket. "Now, let me handle this next part myself, but watch what I do."

Jacob respectfully stood back as Rebecca lifted the box, sharply tapped one corner on the ground to knock the majority of bees to one side, then lifted the box and simply dumped the swarm into the empty hive. She stood back and rested the nearly empty box back on the ground.

"That's it?" he asked, amazed.

"*Ja*, that's it." He could see her smile through the veil. "The queen is somewhere in that mass of worker bees, and as long as she's there, the swarm is likely to stay in the hive. All the rest of the bees left in the box will get themselves oriented within a couple hours and find their way to the hive. Now, let's fit these frames in among the bees. I like to go slow and gentle so I don't squash anyone in the process."

He followed her example as she carefully slid the frames into the hive, moving them slowly so the bees had time to get out of the way.

"I have a *gut* feeling about this," she said at one point. "I can never be sure, of course, but I'm fairly confident this swarm will stay in the hive."

"Has a swarm ever left after you put them into a hive?"

"*Ja* sure. It happened twice last year. You can't force bees to stay when they want to go. That's why I try to do everything possible to make their new home as inviting as I can."

Once the frames were in place, Rebecca hunted on the ground until she found a small stick. "I'll put the cover on the hive, but prop it up just a bit with this stick," she explained. "It will help any stray bees find their way. I'll remove the stick tomorrow. The box and the sheet will stay here throughout the day, and I'll pick them up tonight."

When the hive cover was in place, Jacob stood back

with Rebecca and watched as bees buzzed around the new hive. She unzipped her veil and let it hang down the back of her bee suit, and he followed suit. The other hives, he noticed, were becoming more active as well, since the sun was now shining on them.

He glanced around the bee yard. "I have a lot to learn if I'm going to take these over," he murmured almost to himself.

Rebecca shot him a sharp look. "What do you mean?"

"I mean..." He trailed off for a moment, groping for a diplomatic way to phrase it.

"You mean if I leave this job?" Rebecca seemed to pluck his thought out of the air. She shook her head. "The bees are mine. They'll go with me."

Jacob nearly staggered back. "I thought they were Caleb's."

"Nein." Her eyes were cold. "I'm the one who purchased the equipment and the first colonies. All the hives are mine. These bees aren't just any bees. These are bees I've spent the last five years breeding specifically to be resistant to varroa mites. If I go, they come with me." She spun on her heel and stalked off toward the barn.

Jacob stared after her. He wanted the bees. They were an integral part of the plans he had for the farm. So...if the bees were hers, it looked like he was stuck with her.

For the time being.

He peeled himself out of the bee suit and carried it over one arm as he headed back to the house. He knew Rebecca was in the barn doing the morning chores, and didn't feel like trespassing on her temper at the moment. Instead, he entered the house through the outside kitchen door and found Caleb cracking eggs into a bowl. *"Guder mariye."*

"Guder mariye," the older man replied. He had a cheery look on his face. "I saw you and Rebecca in the bee yard. Were you hiving the swarm?"

"*Ja.* She says she's confident they'll stay."

"That's *gut,*" he said as he began beating the eggs vigorously with a fork. "It's nice to see you and Rebecca working so well together."

Jacob grunted but didn't want to burst the older man's bubble. He was sure Caleb knew whom the bees belonged to, but didn't feel like delving into the possibility of Rebecca departing along with all the hives.

Instead, he replied neutrally, "*Ja*, she knows a lot. I'm interested in how the hives work. I'll have to learn as much as I can from her."

"Well, there's time." Caleb poured the beaten eggs into a pan. "I'm glad you two seem to have set aside your differences."

"I wouldn't go that far." Jacob hung the bee suit on a hook near the door. "She's still prickly and takes offense easily. Honestly, Uncle Caleb, I think she doesn't want me here at all."

"That may be." Caleb seemed undisturbed by the thought. "But you're both mature adults. You'll find ways to work with each other. Meanwhile, I've been giving more thought to staying in Montana and living here in a *daadi haus*. I admit the idea has some appeal."

"Just say the word and I'll start building one." As

pleased as he was at the prospect of Caleb staying in Montana, his mind kept returning to Rebecca.

He realized his position had shifted in a subtle way. A few minutes ago, he was the boss. He was the one who stood poised to inherit the farm. Rebecca had no negotiating power beyond her years of loyalty to Caleb.

But now she had a bargaining chip in her favor: she owned the bees and the hives. It was a powerful weapon, and one she clearly hadn't hesitated to wield.

So for the moment it seemed he had two choices: either he could learn everything possible about bees and try to start his own hives right away…or he could put up with Rebecca's attitude and prickly feelings, and do what he could not to chase her away.

With a feeling of gloom, he knew what he had to do.

Chapter Nine

After lunch, Rebecca was just about to head for the garden to do some weeding when Jacob stopped her.

"I'm going to be adding to the new garden space," he said. "I could use an extra pair of hands."

"*Ja* sure." Her words were automatic, but then she paused. Did she really want to work on a project with Jacob? A small inner voice scolded her, *You do if you want to keep your job.*

She mentally shrugged. Jacob was now part of Caleb's farm whether she liked it or not. Besides, she was curious about what he planned to do with the new garden space.

"Let's move the chicken tractor first," he suggested as they left the house and walked toward the garden. "I want to see how much they've scratched up."

For the next several hours, he kept her busy. Together they trundled the chicken tractor to a new location, and then moved and spread compost over a new section of ground.

"It's a long-term process," he explained as they worked. "Permaculture is not something that is built up in a year, but over several years. However, once things are in place, as much as possible it starts to mimic the way nature does things, so going forward it's mostly maintenance-free."

"But how can a farm turn a profit if it doesn't grow crops?" she asked, raking an area.

"It *will* grow crops," he countered. "Just not in large fields of monoculture. In some ways, Caleb's farm is the perfect size. It's not so big that it dwarfs what I want to try, and it's not so small that it won't provide enough produce to turn a profit."

He went on and on, explaining enthusiastically about his ideas, and Rebecca listened. She began to understand he didn't want to dismantle the work she and Caleb had done, so much as supplement it. Despite herself, she was fascinated.

"How did you get involved in this newfangled farming technique?" she asked.

"I attended a day-long seminar," he replied. "I learned that small-scale farming doesn't have to mean years of backbreaking labor. Permaculture nurtures the soil, it creates happy livestock and it provides meat, eggs, fruits and vegetables that everyone demands—all for less work." He stopped and gazed over the farm for a moment, a faraway look in his eyes. "I watched my father struggle to maintain the difficult work schedule as he got older, and I recognized there's an easier way to keep a farm running than working oneself into the ground."

"That's why there are *daadi hauses*," she replied. "So the older people don't have to work as hard, and the younger people can take over the burden."

"*Ja* sure, but my youngest *bruder* wasn't old enough to take over the farm until my *daed* had worked himself too hard. There had to be an easier way, and I think permaculture is the answer."

"But you said you were working for your older *bruder* on his farm, and he wasn't interested in incorporating anything you suggested?"

"*Ja.* My older brother is a *gut* man, but stubborn. He wanted things done his way. I guess I'm stubborn, too, and wanted to try things *my* way. That's why Caleb's offer of this farm is such a blessing."

"I can see why the bees are part of your plans," she remarked at last.

He grinned. "*Ja.* Having such a concentration of pollinators is a huge benefit. And I'm glad," he added, "that I won't have to learn the intricacies of beekeeping right away, since a resident expert already lives here."

She glanced at him. He was watching her with an enigmatic expression.

"So you're not kicking me off the property?" she ventured.

"Nein," he replied. "You told me yourself if you leave, the bees go with you. I don't want to lose the bees."

"Nice to be wanted," she said sarcastically, and turned back to her raking. But she was pleased. If Jacob wanted to keep her around because of the bees, she didn't mind. It meant she could stay on this farm she had come to love so well. It meant she didn't have to move all of her hives. It meant she didn't have to find a new place to live and work.

"Speaking of *daadi hauses*," said Jacob after a few minutes' silence, "Caleb said he's been thinking, and the idea of staying here in Pierce has some appeal. He hasn't made up his mind, but it seems more likely."

She straightened up and smiled at him. "Oh, that would be *wunnerschee*!" she exclaimed. "I dreaded the thought of him leaving."

"Well, he hasn't entirely agreed yet," Jacob said. "But I'm working on it. Being around him again makes me realize how much I loved that man while growing up. Maybe it's because he and Naomi couldn't have kids, but he was always the most *wunnerschee* uncle."

"The whole church loves him here," Rebecca added. "He's like a grandfather to everyone. All the *kinner* know he's *gut* for a story or perhaps some candy."

"So how did you end up answering Caleb's advertisement in *The Budget*, anyway?" Jacob asked as he spread more compost.

She debated for a few moments, then decided to tell him the truth. "I was escaping the matchmaking of my *mamm* and *tante*," she confessed. "My mother and her sister's favorite hobby is to get all the young people in the church married off." She paused. "It didn't work for me."

"What happened?" he asked.

She shrugged. "My betrothed got cold feet at the last minute and left the community for an *Englisch* job shortly before we got married. Essentially he left me at the altar, though not quite as dramatically."

"You're kidding." Jacob jerked upright and stared at her.

"*Nein*, I'm not kidding." She could feel her cheeks flare with heat. "It was humiliating beyond belief. I told *Mamm* I'd had enough of her meddling in my love life. But as embarrassing as it was for me, it was worse for my best friend, Leah. She actually *did* marry the man my mother and aunt set her up with. It breaks my heart to see how unhappy she is."

He winced. "I'm so sorry to hear that. Is he abusive?"

"*Nein*, they're just not very compatible. Now she's stuck with him for life. I think it was a blessing in disguise when Jeremiah dumped me."

"So you answered an advertisement for a farm hand?"

"*Ja*. I'm surprised Caleb hired me instead of a strapping young man, but I think he was under the impression he was rescuing a damsel in distress when I explained about my *mamm*'s matchmaking. I'm more grateful than I can say to be here in Montana instead of back in Indiana."

She didn't say anything about Caleb's own matchmaking inclinations between her and Jacob. However, she was no longer an impressionable young woman. With age came wisdom…*and* confidence. Never again would she be pushed into something she didn't want to do…especially if it came with lifelong repercussions.

As for Jeremiah, she'd heard rumors that he'd worked for a while in the *Englisch* world and then moved to another town and joined the church there. And she didn't much care. Even now, five years later, his actions still stung and she wanted no reminder of either her own youthful folly, or her mother's insistence that marriage was the only goal she should have in life.

She glanced across the farm toward the bee yard. In some ways, her millions of honeybees had taken on a deeper significance than merely a productive apiary. They had taken the place of a husband. It was a lot to ask of a group of insects, but for the time being she was satisfied.

Jacob was the first fly in her ointment, but since he had just said she could stay where she was, she renewed her determination to prove her worth.

As for Caleb…while she desperately hoped the older man accepted Jacob's offer to live in a *daadi haus*, she was determined not to let him push her into any unwanted relationship with his great-nephew.

Of all the reasons he speculated why Rebecca wasn't married at the age of twenty-eight, being left at the altar was the last thing Jacob imagined. Such drama was rare among the Amish. Or was there another reason he dumped her?

Subtly, he glanced at her as she worked nearby. Her *kapp* was tidy, her dark brown hair was neatly confined beneath except for a few stray wisps. She wore a burgundy dress with a black apron, and she had a smudge of dirt on one cheek.

She was a complicated woman. If Caleb hoped a spark of affection would ignite between them, the old man was going to be disappointed.

On the other hand, Jacob did admire Rebecca. He could understand Caleb's affection for her. Keeping her around simply to maintain the bees wouldn't be so much of a hardship after all.

To his surprise, she piped up with a question. "You're the same age I am," she remarked. "Why aren't you married?"

He grunted. "I wanted to be. I courted a girl years ago, but didn't have anything to offer. No farm. No way to support a family while working for my brother."

"What happened to the girl?"

"She married someone else. She's very happy as far as I know. Has two kids. It's like…it's like everyone was ahead of me in their life's plans. It was very frustrating. I saved every penny I could, but property is scarce in Ohio since it's so crowded. I knew I couldn't court anyone until my circumstances changed. That's yet another reason I'm so grateful to Caleb for this inheritance."

"Well, now that you're here, you should look over the community's inventory of available women and pick one," Rebecca teased. "There's a young widow, Grace Eicher, who might suit you. She has no children and is very pretty."

"I thought you didn't approve of matchmaking," he remarked.

Her cheeks flushed. "*Ja*, you're right. Besides, Grace is even more stubborn than I am, so you'd probably not suit each other."

He chuckled. He didn't know who this Grace Eicher was, but he doubted anyone could be more stubborn than Rebecca.

And yet…when they were working together like this, he found Rebecca enjoyable to be around. She was an admirable listener. She asked intelligent questions. She was astoundingly knowledgeable about the farm and her bees. He wondered…

No. No courtship. She didn't seem to want it, and Jacob himself didn't appreciate Caleb's hints in that direction.

"Look at that." He pointed to a flower. A honeybee had landed on its petals and was creeping toward the center. "I see bees everywhere. It's *wunnerschee*. You must have noticed a huge uptick in the amount of food production after getting the hives."

"*Ja.*" She, too, paused to watch the bee, a smile hovering on her lips. "I read something recently about urban farming, how people were planting vegetable plots in vacant lots, that kind of thing. A beekeeper came along and started putting hives near the vacant lots, and the productivity of the gardens exploded tenfold."

"I've heard about urban gardening." Jacob pitched some compost. "It's a nice trend."

"*Ja*, it is. But that article illustrated how important pollinators are. I have people asking me if I can put hives on their property for that reason. It would be a lot of work, though—not just to move the hives, but to maintain them if they're scattered far and wide. And it's just me working the bees."

"What if you had another person to help?" Jacob asked. It occurred to him that providing pollination services across the settlement wasn't a bad side gig.

"*Ja*, that might work," she replied, returning to her raking. "But there's no one else I've found."

"If you offered pollination services, would you use your own hives, or try to establish new hives?" he asked.

"Hmm. I'm not sure." She stopped raking and rubbed her chin. "I've almost got too many hives in one spot now. There's something to be said for spreading them out to other farms on the settlement."

"I could help you do that, you know," he said quietly.

Rebecca snapped her head around and stared. "What?"

"You got me interested in honeybees," he replied with a half smile. "I blame you for this. But honestly, if some others in the church want a hive or two on their property, I could help. It could become a sideline business."

"J-ja," she stuttered. "You remember when Ephraim King said he wanted bees? He's not the only one who's said that. People have offered to pay. I'd have to look up what might be reasonable to charge. Are you serious, Jacob? I had thought about offering pollination services before, but knew I couldn't do it alone."

"Then why don't we start it as a small sideline business? We can split any income that comes in. We can also split the maintenance once the hives are in place on other properties."

She rubbed the back of her neck. "This is so sudden, it will take some thinking through. But I know it would be a success. For two or three years now, people in church have expressed interest in having hives on their farms, so all we'd have to do is put the word out and we'd have as many locations as we'd want."

"Is this a *gut* time of year to move hives?"

"Spring? *Ja*, couldn't be better, for a number of reasons. One, the hives are lighter to lift up since they're not heavy with honey. For another, there are a lot of spring flowers, so the bees will have food sources right away."

"So it's settled, then. We have a new business."

She looked a little dazed, then laughed. "*Ja*, I guess we have a new business."

"Besides putting the word out, what should be the first step to move a hive?"

"I'm not sure. I have some bee books in my cabin, so I'll have to look it up. I think I remember reading they need to be able to identify their hive in the new location, so using color is a big help. You remember how some of the hives are painted in different colors? We could move those first."

"*Ja gut.* And what if I installed a painted board right in front of the hive entrance? Like a landing board? That way they'd get used to identifying the new hive as theirs."

"Have you been secretly reading up on bees?" she asked in a teasing voice.

"*Nein*, but I wouldn't mind doing that. If you have any books you could lend me, I could do some research."

Rebecca hugged herself. "A new business. This might work, Jacob!"

He laughed. "*Ja*, it's exciting."

What he didn't want to admit was how Rebecca was transformed in that moment. He had never seen her so purely happy before. Her dark eyes sparkled, her body language was animated, her smile was beautiful.

"I have some leftover paint from a couple years ago

still sitting in the barn," she mused after a moment, resuming her raking. "I don't know what kind of condition it's in, but it doesn't have to be anything fancy for entrance boards."

"I can make some boards this afternoon," he replied, pitching some compost to a new area. "They can be ready to paint tomorrow. How should we let church members know about hives?"

"Word of mouth will do the trick. I can get some flyers printed up in town and we can hand them out and ask people to spread the word. I'll leave a stack at the Yoders' store in town, too, and ask Mabel and Abe to give them to church members. For now, I think it would be best to just keep the hives on the settlement rather than scatter them farther afield out of town."

"Ja gut," he replied. He grinned, pleased with the whole idea—both of starting a new sideline business, and also, to his surprise, having a reason to work more closely with Rebecca.

"Eva Hostetler is *gut* at sketching and drawing. Maybe she can design the flyers," she said. "If we start preparing right away, we should be ready to move hives within a couple weeks." She leaned her rake against the cart. "In fact, I'm going to go check whether that paint in the barn is still any good."

He also leaned his pitchfork against the cart, catching her enthusiasm. "And I'll see what kind of wood is available for landing boards for the hives."

She grinned. "And after that, let's go figure out which hives we want to use for this project."

"You're on."

Her grin widened. "You know what, Jacob? You're not so bad when you're not trying to kick me off the farm."

He snorted in amusement. "And you're not so bad when you're talking about your bees."

"Let's go!"

Chapter Ten

The paint was usable. It wasn't in the best condition, but the leftover quarts of pale blue, pink and yellow would suit for painting landing boards for beehives. Pleased, Rebecca left Jacob to rummage in the woodshop portion of the barn and headed for the bee yard.

As always, the industry among the colonies in the yard calmed her. And at the moment, she needed calming.

She and Jacob had turned a corner. That much was obvious. Not only had they gotten to know each other better, but they were also planning a side business to work on together.

Truth be told, she was trying her best not to change her thinking about Jacob from adversary to ally—yet that's exactly what had happened. She couldn't start a pollination business with an adversary. She *could* start a side business with an ally.

She and Jacob would be working even more closely together. She didn't know whether to be pleased or terrified at the thought.

Long ago, Rebecca had reconciled herself to being single. After what happened to poor Leah—and her own close escape from what would undoubtedly have been a similarly unhappy marriage—she had no desire to put her neck in that noose, even if it meant never having a family.

Yet here she was, working alongside an eligible man her own age. It didn't take a genius to understand why Caleb had matchmaking on his mind for her and Jacob.

Could she release the resentment she'd harbored and open herself to the thought of courtship? Did she *want* courtship? Did she *want* marriage?

In theory, yes. In reality…she wasn't sure. She was used to being independent. That was hard to give up.

She could almost hear her mother's voice, scolding about her unmarried state and hinting that fulfillment could only come from being a wife and mother. The trouble was, Rebecca was so used to pushing back against her mother's nagging that she was suppressing her own longing for marriage and motherhood.

Rebecca lifted her head and looked around the bee yard. Instead of seeking out a *hutband,* she had focused on her beehives. For five years, these insects had dominated her thoughts.

But were they enough?

From the corner of her eye, something caught her attention. She turned, and her jaw dropped. Then she felt the blood drain from her face.

A bear was approaching the bee yard. In all the years she'd lived in Montana, she had never seen a bear—and yet this one was walking right toward her, cautiously, glancing between her and the abundance of hives.

It had never occurred to her how vulnerable her precious hives could be, subject to the whims of powerful and omnivorous wildlife such as bears. It was a smorgasbord for the animal, a simple matter of deciding which delicious treasure trove to destroy first in his quest for both honey and brood.

Rebecca wasn't about to let a bear demolish all her hives, along with all the years of hard work and careful breeding that went into them. Looking around frantically for rocks or something she could throw, she saw the sturdy garden rake left behind when she and Jacob had leveled the ground for the new hive. She dashed over, snatched up the tool and ran toward the bear, brandishing the rake.

"Get out!" she screamed. "Scat! Go!"

Caught by surprise, the bear jerked to a stop. Then, as Rebecca continued to run toward him, screaming and waving the rake, the animal backed up, turned and fled into the woods.

Blinded as she was by her fury, she didn't hear anything else but the blood pounding in her ears. It wasn't until she felt her arm grabbed that she stopped her charge.

"Are you delirious?" shouted Jacob. He gripped her arm hard.

Panting, she wheeled on him. "Leave me alone! He's not going to get my bees!"

"*Nein!* You're not chasing a bear. It's dangerous!" His eyes snapped fire at her.

"He won't get my bees! I won't let him!"

"Rebecca, *stop*!" he roared.

Startled out of her single-minded fury by his bellow, she stared at him. For a moment, silence crackled between them.

"What were you thinking, chasing a bear?" he yelled. "It could easily have turned on you."

"I won't let a bear destroy five years' worth of hard work," she snapped. She set the rake against the log again at the opposite end of the bee yard.

Then the adrenaline left her system, and she all but collapsed onto the log, trembling violently. She had just *chased a bear* away from the hives. A bear. What was she thinking? The trembling increased, her body shaking so hard her teeth clacked.

Suddenly she felt herself being pulled into Jacob's arms as he straddled the log beside her. He simply held her, allowing the delayed reaction to the fear to run its course.

"I was terrified," he whispered against her *kapp*. "I saw the bear come out of the woods and was just about to shout when you went after him. I raced over here as fast as I could. What made you think you could chase him off?"

"I d-didn't th-think it th-through," she spluttered. "I was j-just so m-mad at the th-thought of him d-destroying the hives..."

"The hives aren't worth your life."

"E-easy to s-say..."

"They're not."

It took a few moments for Rebecca to realize the significance of what was happening. Jacob held her close, soothing her, calming her. She felt protected in his arms—protected and safe, from everything…including bears.

Confused, she drew away from the forbidden comfort he offered. As a poor substitute, she fished a handkerchief from her pocket and buried her face in it. She wasn't crying, exactly, but she felt weepy.

"Are you sure you're *oll recht*?" asked Jacob after a few moments.

"*Ja.* Just… It's just hitting me what I did. You're right, it was a dumb thing to do. I j-just didn't think, I only a-acted."

"Don't do it again, okay? I don't like the feeling of having five years of my life scared out of me."

She glanced at him and saw an expression of teasing concern on his face. She didn't want to analyze that expression too closely. "*Nein*, I won't do that again. But…" She glanced around at the bee yard. "But I'm going to have to build a fence. I won't risk having that bear come back, now that he knows where the hives are."

"*Ja*, a fence is a *gut* idea." Jacob, too, looked around the bee yard. "I saw some rolls of deer netting in the barn. Would that work?"

"I'm not sure." Rebecca considered the area. "But maybe if the deer netting is reinforced with field fence."

"Anything is better than nothing." Jacob got off the log and held out a hand to help her up. "No time like the present. If we can at least get the deer netting up tonight, we can finish installing the rest of it by tomorrow."

"We?" Rebecca rested her hand in his as she rose to

her feet, then dropped her hand by her side. Touching Jacob, however politely, was still too personal for her. It was disconcerting enough that she had actually leaned into him for comfort. "The bees are mine, and so are the problems. There's no need for you to help with the fencing. I can handle it."

"I'm sure you can, but two can get it done twice as fast."

"Then, *danke*. I won't argue."

She turned to lead the way toward the barn. She was glad for activity, glad for an excuse to rummage for supplies and equipment in the barn without having to consider the feeling of comfort and security he had given her.

"These T-posts belong to Caleb, but I hope he won't mind if I use them," she commented, motioning to a pile of extra-long fence posts. "I can replace them later if he needs them. I've got some ear protection, and Caleb has two post pounders."

"And gloves," added Jacob. He fished two pairs from a bin. "Let me get a hand truck, and we can start moving posts."

The next few hours were busy. Rebecca and Jacob donned ear protection, then each took a heavy metal post pounder and slammed the pounder over and over to drive the T-posts into the ground. The work was exhausting, but nothing she hadn't done before.

"I just want to get at least the deer netting up by tonight," she said wearily, bending over and bracing her hands on her knees to catch her breath. "I'm half tempted to spend the night here to make sure the bear doesn't come back."

"You'll do no such thing," Jacob growled. He wiped off a bead of sweat trickling down the side of his face. "But I think if we just space the T-posts twice as wide as they should be, then string out the deer netting, it will at least discourage the bear. We can finish up and do a better job tomorrow." He squinted at the lowering sun. "We didn't tell Caleb what we're doing. I hope he doesn't mind cooking dinner tonight."

"We might be eating it cold. I don't want to stop." Rebecca hoisted the post pounder in one hand and picked up another T-post with the other. "Back to work."

The sun was nearly setting by the time they unwound the tall deer netting and strung it clumsily around the perimeter of the bee yard, but when at last she and Jacob stood back to examine their handiwork, she was moderately pleased. "If nothing else, hopefully it will hinder the bear for one night," she said. Then she turned and faced Jacob squarely. "*Vielen dank* for helping. It would have devastated me to lose my hives to a bear. I couldn't have done this without you."

He smiled, a genuine smile that lit up his face. "We're business partners now, don't forget. I have a vested interest in making sure we have hives to loan out for pollination." He wiped his face with a handkerchief and pocketed it, then held out the crook of his arm. "Let's go get something to eat. I'm starving, and I'm sure you must be, too."

Without objection, Rebecca linked arms with him and they walked toward the farmhouse.

* * *

"*Danke* for making dinner, Uncle," Jacob said, stuffing his mouth with a biscuit as Caleb sat opposite him at the kitchen table. "And for keeping it warm for us, too."

"I saw you both out there working frantically on the fence and guessed something was amiss, and figured what you both needed was a hot meal instead of an old man getting in the way." Caleb beamed at him and Rebecca. "And I'll do the dishes tonight. I suspect you're both exhausted."

"Ja, danke," said Rebecca in a heartfelt voice.

She reached for the butter and Jacob saw her wince. "Muscles tightening up?" he asked in sympathy.

"Ja." She sighed. "I feel drained. But I would have been a lot more exhausted without your help."

Her admission of gratitude was unusual. From the corner of his eye, Jacob saw Caleb glance sharply at Rebecca. He deliberately kept his own face impassive. "We've got more to do tomorrow."

"And I trust you won't be chasing any more bears." Caleb gave a rusty chuckle. "Though it doesn't surprise me to hear you did that, *liebling*. I can't decide if it was brave or foolish to run it off."

"Definitely foolish," Jacob chimed in before Rebecca could answer. "If it had come after you, what would you have done?"

"Best not to think about it," inserted Caleb hastily. "Just keep doing what you're doing, which is to fence the bee yard."

"I think, if we're going to put hives on other properties, we'd better fence them in, too," Jacob said thoughtfully.

"Hives on other properties?" Caleb said in bewilderment.

Rebecca chuckled. "So much has happened that I forgot to mention it, Caleb. Jacob and I are thinking about a sideline business renting out hives for pollination purposes. You know how many people from church have already asked. Ephraim King specifically asked for some. We were just going to do some of the prep work when the bear showed up."

"You *and* Jacob, eh?" Caleb chewed his food, a thoughtful expression on his face. "Is that possible without killing each other?" he teased.

"*Ja*, well, we seem to have come to a truce," admitted Jacob. "You never told me she owned the hives, Caleb."

"Makes her more valuable, ain't so?" Caleb winked at Rebecca, who seemed unfazed by the older man's offbeat humor.

Jacob yawned in the middle of his meal. "*Entschuldigung*, excuse me," he apologized. "I suppose I'm more worn out than I want to admit. You must be, too," he added to Rebecca.

"Ja," she said, and wiped a hand over her face. "But I'm pleased we got as much done as we did. I don't know how well I'll sleep tonight, though," she added. "I keep fearing that bear will come back."

"You two have no idea how pleased I am that you're working together," said Caleb. He forked some potatoes into his mouth. "It's important to me. I love you both like the children I never had, and I don't like seeing my children not getting along. I'll do whatever it takes to encourage that."

Jacob glanced at the older man. There seemed to be a deeper meaning to his words, something that jangled a deeply buried nerve. Or maybe he was just overtired and imagining things.

"I feel the same way, Caleb," replied Rebecca, smiling at him.

"I wish there was a way to officially make you my granddaughter," remarked Caleb. "Short of adopting you, that is."

"*Ja*, adoption at twenty-eight would be strange." Rebecca sipped some iced tea, and her voice was bland.

Jacob wondered if she was still annoyed at being passed over for inheritance.

But the older man's comments bothered Jacob for some reason. What an odd line of thought. He knew Caleb well enough to know he seldom said things that weren't backed up by a strong line of reasoning. Did he have something up his sleeve? Was he planning anything?

Yet, what could Caleb do? Adopt Rebecca? What difference would that make? It was all too much for him to figure out, especially in his exhausted state.

"Well, I'm going to pull the horses and cows into the barn tonight," he replied. "If there are bears prowling around, I don't want them disturbing the livestock."

"I'll take care of the cows," said Rebecca. "I still need to milk anyway."

"And I'll do the dishes," offered Caleb.

"Then I'll take care of the horses and chickens," said Jacob. He finished his dinner and pushed away from the table. "No time like the present, then. I'm going to bed early tonight."

"*Ja*, I want to get the milking done." Rebecca wiped her mouth and placed the napkin on the table. "*Danke* for cooking, Caleb."

While walking out to the barn, Jacob decided to voice his concerns.

"Did you get the impression Caleb was dancing around something at dinner?" he asked.

"You mean that strange comment about adopting me?" Rebecca replied. "*Ja*. That was weird."

"It makes me wonder what he has up his sleeve. It's almost as if he was planning something, but I can't fathom what it might be."

"I suppose one or the other of us could just come right out and ask him," said Rebecca.

Jacob smiled to himself. It was so typical of Rebecca's nature—forthright, blunt, direct. "I don't even know what I might ask him. But when he gets that mischievous twinkle in his eye, I suspect he's up to something. Okay, I'm going to go round up the horses. See you in the morning."

But hours later, long after the chores were done and the farm was quiet, Jacob was lying in bed, unable to sleep. His muscles ached, yes, but it was more than that. He stared at the dark ceiling, his mind awhirl.

Over and over he reviewed the day's activities—everything from the excitement he felt at launching a new business with Rebecca, to the terror he experienced as he watched her chase away the bear, to the vague concerns about Caleb's comments.

But foremost—deeper than anything—were the emotions he'd felt when he'd held Rebecca in his arms in the aftermath of the bear encounter. Until now, he hadn't had time to analyze those emotions. Now, in the dark quiet of his bedroom, he took the hidden shining jewel from the pocket of his heart and examined it more closely.

What he saw was disturbing. He realized that Rebecca, as feisty and opinionated as she was, was a woman of rare courage and presence. She wasn't afraid to tell him off, to voice her viewpoints, to act on her convictions.

And she was strong, both physically and mentally. The work they did this afternoon—pounding in so many T-posts—had exhausted him. He could only fathom how much more it had tired her. But she never complained, never slowed down and kept up with him, post for post. He wondered if aching muscles were keeping her awake as much as his were.

Restless in bed, he found himself wondering about the man who had courted her then dumped her so close to the wedding date. What had scared him off? What did that man know that he didn't know? Clearly, it had hurt her beyond what she'd admitted to him, and had scared her off from not just matchmaking, but marriage. At age twenty-eight, he wondered if she would ever marry.

And if so, *whom* she would marry.

That's one thing Caleb had already mentioned about this newish Montana Amish community. People who were single tended not to stay single for long. A lot of people were moving to Montana from overcrowded churches back east. Most had families, but some were single young adults. Caleb's age was an exception; most older people didn't want to leave their families and all that was familiar behind.

Caleb had mentioned that whenever a younger unmarried person came to town, they were usually married within a year. But not Rebecca.

The independent streak that caused her to move away from her family and friends in Indiana likely meant there was more to her story than she'd let on. She'd hinted at a falling-out with her mother, which was part of it. But there seemed to be other factors, too. Her former fiancé, the friend whose marriage was unhappy and, of course, the meddling mother and aunt evidently combined into a powerful force that had sent her out into the unknown lands of the Montana settlement.

And yet, though she had been here five years, she was still unmarried. He had to wonder why.

Because one thing was becoming clear: with the least bit of encouragement, his interest in her could take a turn for something more serious.

He wished he could do something for her, something that might make her smile. But what?

Before drifting off to sleep, he had a thought that sent a smile to his lips.

Yes, he knew what he could do to make her smile. Tomorrow, he would surprise her.

Chapter Eleven

Rebecca woke up to the sound of metal banging on metal. She rolled over, trying to analyze what the sound was, and groaned in pain. Every muscle hurt from her stubborn determination to match Jacob when they'd pounded in the posts yesterday afternoon.

Metal banging on metal—that was the sound of a post pounder banging another T-post into the ground. She peered at the clock. It was barely six in the morning and the sun wasn't even up yet, though the sky was light. What was Jacob doing, working at this hour?

She stumbled out of bed and went through her morning ablutions, slipping a clean apron over her work dress and pinning her *kapp* over her hair. Then she emerged into a sparkling fresh morning and made her way toward the sound.

Jacob was working on the fencing around the bee yard, wearing ear protection as he focused on pounding in another T-post. Even more, he had tidied up the hasty job they had done the night before, extended the height of the T-posts with wood pieces to brace the tall deer netting and reinforced the deer netting with field fencing.

Had he been up all night working? How had he accomplished so much? The fence looked much more sturdy and professional.

She stood in the shadow of a tree, watching. She was coming to appreciate that when Jacob focused on a project, he gave it everything he had. Though the morning was cool, she could see a sheen of sweat on his brow and dampness on his shirt. He finished banging in a T-post on one side of what she now saw was a gate. He dropped the heavy post pounder to the ground, removed his ear protection and fished out a handkerchief to wipe his face.

He was doing this for her. Though he might claim he was just protecting his investment in their new business venture, he knew how much the hives meant to her.

Just then, a thought flashed through her mind. Long ago, when she was a *youngie*, her grandmother had mentioned how men show affection. "They don't like to *talk*," she'd told Rebecca. "They like to *act*. Men show affection by *doing* things."

Somewhere in the back of her mind, Rebecca had tucked away that brief conversation without giving it much thought. Now, as she watched Jacob work so hard to strengthen the fence around the beehives, she suddenly understood her grandmother's words.

Did this mean he was showing affection? To her?

She wasn't sure she was ready for such a conclusion. All these years, she thought she was satisfied with her single status, never tempted by any man, and yet it seemed Jacob was trying to prove something to her.

To be sure, their acrimonious relationship had improved, helped along by Caleb's encouragement. But if Jacob was showing affection by working on the beeyard fence to please her, she wasn't sure what to think… or how to react.

Knowing she couldn't linger in the shadow of the pines all morning, she stepped into the light and walked toward him.

It was a few moments before he saw her. *"Guder mariye,"* he said.

"Guder mariye," she replied. "Did you work all night on this?"

"*Nein*, just got up early. My muscles were sore," he admitted, and gifted her with a smile so dazzling that her knees went weak. "I didn't sleep well."

"I'm sore, too, but I slept like a rock." She gestured toward the fence. "Apparently what we did yesterday afternoon worked well enough to keep the bear out overnight, and what you've done looks *wunnerschee*. And a gate, too! *Danke*, Jacob."

"For sure and certain, I can't see how a bear could get through this." He stepped back and glanced at his handiwork. "I think I've thought of a way to make a miniaturized version of this when we rent out hives on other properties, too."

Maybe she was wrong. Maybe Jacob was only interested in protecting his investment in their business venture. She tamped down on anything that resembled disappointment, and strove to be positive. "And I'm going to go into town today and get some flyers made, then drop a stack off at Yoder's Mercantile in town."

"I've heard about the store from church members, but I haven't been there yet."

She was surprised. "You haven't? Oh, it's the nicest store. Abe and Mabel Yoder opened it a few years ago, and it's become one of the most popular places in town, even for *Englischers*, who like the coffee shop and the bakery. You should come with me," she added, inviting him on impulse.

"*Ja gut*, I'd like that." He tested the strength of the T-post supporting the gate by giving it a little shake. "I think this will hold. Now it's time for chores. I've got to release the horses and chickens. Do you need help with the milking?"

"*Nein*, I'll take care of it. I'll ask Caleb if he needs anything from town, and we can go in after lunch."

Walking away to start her morning chores, she fought off a feeling of satisfaction. It would be fun showing Jacob the tiny town of Pierce, which had been so welcoming to their new Amish neighbors.

"*Ja*, I wouldn't mind some lemons," said Caleb after lunch, when asked if he might need something from town. "And some fresh ginger."

Rebecca nodded as she laid a sheet of paper on the table. "Here are the flyers I designed. Let me know if I should add anything."

Jacob and Caleb bent over the paper, examining it. The sheet had bold lettering, a listed price for summer beehive rentals and a crude drawing of a beehive.

"Looks *gut* to me," said Jacob after a moment.

"*Ja,* me, too." Caleb smiled at her. "Your sketch of a hive isn't bad."

"I might have Eva Hostetler draw me a nicer version at some point," replied Rebecca. "She's a true artist. But this gets the point across, and hopefully we can start distributing hives next week."

At that moment, Caleb got up and made to go wash the dishes.

"Oh, no, you've been cooking the last few meals. It's my turn," protested Rebecca.

Caleb waved a hand. "Go on, off with you two. Just don't forget my lemons."

After gathering her flyer and some money, Rebecca walked with Jacob toward the barn, where the buggy was stored.

"I've got to get out more," remarked Jacob, as he began hitching the horse to the buggy. "To think I've been here for a couple weeks and haven't really seen town, except when Caleb picked me up at the bus stop."

"You'll like Pierce. It's a nice place." Rebecca climbed into the buggy after Jacob led the horse and rig out of the barn, then he stepped up and took the reins.

The day was clouding over and it looked like it might rain later on. "Typical spring weather," she pointed out. "It means the bees won't be active. They tend to hole up in inclement weather."

"Does that mean we should wait for rain before moving some hives?" asked Jacob, directing the horse onto the side road passing Caleb's farm.

"Nein," she replied. "Bad weather makes them grumpy.

The best time to move them is after a nice warm afternoon, when they've gone into the hive for the night."

Jacob chuckled. "I didn't know bees could get grumpy."

"If that bear had gotten into a hive, you would have seen a lot of classic grumpy behavior," she retorted. "Not just from the hive he was attacking, but from other hives as well. Remember how I said bee suits are white because the color is not perceived as a threat? Well, if you wore a bee suit that was dark brown, like a bear, the bees wouldn't be nearly as docile when working with them. In fact, they'd attack you quite ferociously. To them, you would just be a two-footed bear."

"They're a lot smarter than I would have given them credit for," he said thoughtfully.

"Honeybees are some of the most wondrous creatures *Gott* ever created," she said seriously. "I don't know why more people in the church haven't gotten interested in them."

"Well, if they start getting hives on their farms, that might change."

"Ja," she said. "You're right. I'm excited by this new business idea, Jacob. The more people who appreciate bees, the better."

"Well, you're the best ambassador," he replied, offering her a cheeky smile. "Enthusiastic *and* pretty."

She was so stunned at his words that she stared at him. However, he continued watching the road and didn't look at her.

"I-I'm not p-pretty," she stuttered at last. "All you have to do is ask Jeremiah."

* * *

Jacob was stunned by her reaction. Had her betrothed dumped her because he thought she wasn't attractive enough? What a heartless cad.

"Is that why he left you?" he asked gently. "Because he didn't like the way you looked?"

"Th-that's what I heard. I never spoke to him directly after he left the community to work in the *Englisch* world. But my friend Leah said she heard through the grapevine that was his reason. Or at least his excuse."

Jacob kept his eyes on the road, but he was aware of her rigid posture, as if she was literally bottling up the humiliation of that incident. "It sounds like you dodged a bullet," he offered. "I can't imagine such a man would have made a *gut hutband*."

"*Ja*. I know that now, though it took some time to recover from the blow. Now I thank *Gott* he left. But it's not what any woman wants to hear." She added in a dry tone, "It damaged my pride."

"I can see why. But I hope that wasn't what scared you away from the idea of marriage."

"That's none of your business," she retorted with heat. "My reasons are my own."

"*Ja*, you're right. But I still think your old betrothed was a fool."

"I won't argue with that." She sighed. "I just wish my *mamm* and *tante* hadn't been so insistent that he was the right man for me. They couldn't have been more wrong."

"I'm sure they meant well."

"Maybe so, but the end result could have been disastrous. That's one of the many reasons I love Caleb so much—he rescued me from a very awkward situation and allowed me to rebuild my life here in Montana."

"*Ja*, Caleb is one of a kind." Jacob paused and added, "And he's a *gut* listener."

"Oh, he had to listen to me a *lot* when I first arrived in Montana," she agreed with wry humor. Glancing at him, she then focused on the road ahead. "I think you can understand why I was half expecting him to leave me the farm."

"Maybe so. But I also hope *you* can understand I had nothing whatsoever to do with his decision. For me, it was a true gift from *Gott*."

"I see that now." She shrugged. "It just leaves my future a bit more unsettled than I'm comfortable with."

"Well, the bees are your passport for staying on the farm as long as you want." The words sounded awkward even as he said them.

"But for how long?" She averted her face to watch the passing landscape. "I guess things suddenly seem even more…temporary. I don't want to ever leave the farm. I've grown to love it as my own, which I know is clearly unreasonable. But someday you might marry and want privacy for you and your *fraa*, and I can't blame you."

"Don't borrow trouble," he replied. "Who knows what the future might bring?"

More and more often he was thinking about the future, and for whatever reason, Rebecca seemed to feature largely in those thoughts.

Reins held loosely in his hands, Jacob looked up and saw the town in front of them. "We're getting close. Where is Yoder's Mercantile?"

"Right on Main Street. You can't miss it. They have parking for buggies right in front."

Within a few minutes, Jacob pulled up alongside another horse and buggy and saw a charming storefront with a broad porch. Buckets held bouquets of spring flowers for sale—narcissus and daffodils. It had both stairs and a ramp leading to the main doors.

"We can park here, but I want to walk a couple blocks that way to get copies made of this flyer," said Rebecca as she climbed down from the buggy and pointed. "Do you want to go into Yoder's while I do that? It won't take me long."

"*Ja* sure." Curious about the inside, Jacob secured the horse and climbed the stairs to the store.

It was as charming as Rebecca had claimed. The first thing that hit him was the delectable smells of fresh coffee and baked goods. Jacob glanced around and saw a small café, a play area for very young children and a bakery with glass-fronted displays with a mouthwatering selection. There was a hum of conversation as *Englischer* customers browsed the goods or sat at tables, drinking coffee.

"*Guder nammidaag*, Jacob," said a woman behind him. "First time in the store?"

He turned and saw a plump middle-aged woman. "*Ja*. Mabel Yoder, right?"

"*Ja*. And you've met my *hutband*, Abe." Her husband, who had a long beard, walked over to them.

Jacob shook hands with both. "I haven't seen anyone since the last church service. Rebecca had an errand here in town, and scolded me that I hadn't been in your store yet. I see why everyone speaks so highly of it."

"Danke." Abe Yoder's eyes crinkled as he smiled. "The townspeople have been very *gut* to us."

"Even the bishop likes to stop in once in a while to have a coffee. He's right there." Mabel lifted a hand, and the church leader—who had been watching them—waved in response. "You might join him until Rebecca gets here," the woman added.

"Ja gut." Courtesy demanded he greet the bishop, so Jacob walked over and shook the older man's hand. "*Guder nammidaag*, Bishop."

"Won't you join me?" Samuel Beiler invited, laying down his newspaper. "If you have time."

"*Ja* sure. I'm waiting for Rebecca, who's running an errand down the street." Jacob ordered a drink from the young man working the coffee machines, then pulled out a seat and joined the bishop at his table.

"I was going to ask you to visit anyway, just to see how you're settling in at Caleb's place." Samuel took a sip of his coffee.

"I'm settling in very well, and like what I've seen so far of Montana. I'm also remembering how fond of Caleb I was while growing up. I'm more grateful than I can say that he chose me as his heir."

"Are things better between you and Rebecca these days?"

"Ja, ja." He rubbed his chin. "We seem to have come to a reconciliation. Things are better now."

"*Gut.* I know Caleb thinks the world of her, and she's known throughout the settlement for her bees."

"That's why we're in town today," said Jacob. "She's getting some flyers printed for a new business we're starting, which is to rent out hives for pollination purposes."

"Really!" Samuel's eyes gleamed. "That's a *gut* idea. Rebecca is smart. This should do well." Samuel sipped his drink. "I'm glad you're getting along better. I'm sure it's important to Caleb that you and Rebecca aren't enemies. And, perhaps, someday you can be more than friends."

Jacob eyed the church leader with suspicion. "Meaning…?"

"Meaning I'm an old man who likes to see people happy." Samuel waved a hand dismissively. "*Ach*, pay me no heed. Look, here comes Rebecca now."

Feeling uneasy about the undertones of the bishop's remarks, Jacob turned to see Rebecca engaged in conversation with Mabel Yoder, a stack of flyers in her hands. He saw Mabel nod and take about half the stack, which she placed behind the cash register. Then Rebecca turned and scanned the store, making her way over to the coffee section.

"*Guder nammidaag*, Bishop." Uninvited, she pulled out a chair and sat down. "I assume Jacob has told you about our new little business venture?"

"*Ja*. I think it's a smart idea. May I see?" The bishop pointed to the flyer.

"*Ja* sure. I didn't want to hand them out on Sunday since that's the Lord's day, so I thought Mabel could give them out to church members as she sees them."

Bishop Beiler scanned the flyers. "Let me have a few, too. I can pass them out as I see people."

"*Danke*, Bishop. That would be most helpful." Rebecca handed him a generous portion of the remaining flyers. "I only had fifty copies made. Maybe I should have made more."

"*Nein*, I'm sure this will be plenty. But I wouldn't be surprised if you were able to rent all your hives out, if that's what you want."

"Well, I only have fifty-five hives, and I—that is, *we*—are renting them in pairs, plus I don't want to ship *all* the hives out, so probably we can only take, what, twenty customers, Jacob? That would leave fifteen hives in the bee yard."

"You know more about this than I do," he replied. "But if nothing else, having the hives distributed in many different places means all your eggs aren't in one basket in case a bear gets to them."

"I chased a bear away from the bee yard yesterday," she explained to the bishop.

"Did you now!" The older man's bushy eyebrows shot upward into his hairline. "That was brave."

"*Nein*, it was *schtupid*," retorted Jacob, "but what's done is done."

"Anyway, we're going to put in fencing to protect any rented hives from bears," concluded Rebecca.

"Well, it sounds like you're off to a *gut* start." Bishop Beiler glanced at the clock over the bakery section. "I must go. I have an appointment with the Kings shortly. I'll be sure to leave them a flyer," he added.

"Danke!" said Jacob.

After the bishop had departed, Rebecca said, "I'll get

the lemons and ginger Caleb wanted, then I'll be ready to leave."

"Ja gut," he replied. He watched her walk away, assessing her rather tall figure and her strong features under the modest *kapp.* So now even the bishop was interested in matchmaking? It seemed everyone was trying to push him and Rebecca together.

It was a concept he wasn't completely against. But she was a tough nut to crack. She'd been hurt and humiliated by the circumstances back in Indiana. Trying to convince her to let him court her could take some time.

But time was something he had plenty of. Suddenly feeling more optimistic, he drained his coffee, deposited his mug in the shop's dishwashing bin and went out to unhitch the horse.

He had a farm now. He had a way to support a family. All he needed was a wife to make the vision complete.

Was Rebecca the woman for him?

Chapter Twelve

"That's the last of the hives we can rent out this year." Rebecca unzipped her bee veil and stepped back to assess how well the two hives were fastened in the back of the wagon.

Jacob also unzipped his veil and let the netted headpiece dangle down the back of his suit. "I never expected hive rentals to be so popular."

"And that's just with church members." Rebecca gave him a sunny smile. "Who knew?"

He grinned back, and for a moment Rebecca got lost in the dark blue of his eyes. That momentary feeling of euphoria had happened several times over the last few weeks as she and Jacob had perfected their technique for renting hives.

In fact, renting had become routine. At each new location, they selected a spot in consultation with the farmer, made a clearing for the hive platform, constructed a small fence around it, then returned home until evening. At dusk, when the bees had all returned to their hive for the night, they suited up, blocked off the entrance to the hive, strapped the segments together so nothing would shake loose, lifted the hives into the back of the wagon, strapped them in place so they wouldn't tip over, then transported them to the new location.

The bee yard was two-thirds empty, with forty of the hives now rented out. The bear had never returned—or if it had, it hadn't been able to breach the fencing.

Grunting a bit as he climbed into the wagon seat and took up the reins, Jacob said, "If nothing else, this has been an excellent opportunity to get to know people from church better. Last Sunday, for the first time, I was able to greet a lot of people by name. And I'm looking forward to the barn raising on Saturday."

"*Ja*, nice bunch, aren't they?" Rebecca finished lighting the lanterns on the sides of the wagon against the twilight, then climbed up to sit beside him. "Maybe it's because we're such a mishmash of church members from all over the eastern states, but this Montana settlement has grown very close. The bishop does a *gut* job of managing everyone, too. We've had a lot of work parties over the last five years, since we're still building up the infrastructure. Building a barn is always a fun time."

Jacob clucked to the horse and started the wagon down the road at a walking pace, going slow so as to jar the bees as little as possible. "I see why you like it out here so much," he remarked. "It's not nearly as crowded as Ohio. There's something to be said for Montana's smaller population."

"And wide-open spaces." She gestured toward the high peaks of the Bitterroot Mountains, shadowed since the sun had long since set behind them. The sky lingered in a late-June twilight of purples and dark blues, and even a bit of green. A great horned owl hooted from the darkness of the nearby woods.

"When should we check on the first hives we rented?" he asked.

"Hmm. We should probably check them about every two weeks," she replied. "We don't have to open the hive unless we suspect a problem, but we should observe the activity to make sure the queen is doing her job. Later in the summer, we'll probably add some supers, too."

"The supers are the extra boxes stacked on top where the bees store honey, right?"

"*Ja.* Think of them like storage sheds or little barns. The baby bees are raised in the lower parts of the hive, the extra honey is stored in the upper parts. During a heavy honey year, I've seen other beekeepers stack as many as five supers on top of the hive boxes."

"I like beekeeping," he remarked, guiding the horse to the left at an intersection of gravel roads. "It's addicting."

She smiled at him. "Told you so."

A comfortable silence descended as the horse walked steadily through the dark. To the west, a glow in the sky could be seen from the lights in town, but from this distance on the road of the Amish settlement, all was quiet and dark. The owl hooted again, and from a short distance away, his mate answered the call in a higher pitch. Once in a while, she could see the glow of oil lamps through the window of a farmhouse they passed, but the gravel road was dark and deserted.

"I got a letter from my *tante* Marie a few days ago," she ventured into the quiet. "Scolding me for not being married yet." She and Jacob had a close enough relationship now that they could discuss such things.

Jacob gave a small snort of amusement. "I've never met your aunt, but she does seem to be obsessed with marrying you off," he observed.

"*Ja.* I write back and completely ignore the nagging, and instead tell her all about what's going on with the bees, or some local gossip from church, or what the weather is like. I think it drives her nuts that I don't rise to the bait."

"Are her own children married? Your cousins, that is?"

"*Ja*, all of them. And they all have children. So do all my brothers and sisters. I'm the last holdout—not to mention the youngest—so I guess it's natural that they should push me to marry, even though it's been five years since I moved to Montana."

"And yet it seems you have a decent relationship with your parents and relatives."

"*Ja*, I do. I get a bit annoyed at their persistence sometimes, but they're all *gut* people. Although it helps to be so far away."

"Have they ever visited you here in Montana?"

"*Nein.* I've invited them plenty of times, but no one has come." She gave a low chuckle. "I suspect the only thing that would entice them out here is a wedding. My own."

"I guess they'll be waiting awhile, then."

"*Ja.* Look, they left a lantern burning for us." She pointed toward a light visible through the trees at the farm where the rental hives would be placed.

Jacob directed the horse up the lengthy driveway to where the lantern burned bright from a hook on a porch post.

As they pulled up to the front of the house, Peter Schrock stepped outside, and his wife and six children—ranging in age from a toddler to a young teen—spilled out behind him, eager to watch the proceedings. "Everything all right?" Peter asked.

"Ja," replied Rebecca. "We'll settle the hives in, and check back in two weeks or so to make sure the bees are doing okay. The children aren't allowed inside the little fenced area, *oll recht*?"

"*Ja.* Can we watch as you move the hives into place?"

"Of course."

Jacob directed the horse toward the area where the hives would be set up as the Schrock family followed in their wake, carrying a lantern and chattering with excitement.

"No one should come any closer than about here," said Rebecca, indicating a spot about ten feet outside the small fenced area. "And once we remove the blockage from the hive entrance, everyone should stay well away. It's not normal for bees to fly at night, but they will if they feel they're being attacked."

The family settled into respectful silence as she and Jacob pulled their veiled headgear back over their heads and zipped the protective attire into place. Then, working with the fluidity that came with several weeks of experience, they carried the hives to the platforms, settled them in place, removed the straps that had held the box sections together, unplugged the entrance holes and retreated. A few bees spilled out angrily, but it was too dark for them to be defensive. Jacob secured the fence behind them as they walked away from the hives.

"That's it," Jacob told the Schrock family, unzipping his veil. "Assuming nothing goes wrong, you'll have bees all over your garden and orchard tomorrow."

"*Ach*, that's *gut*!" exclaimed Peter. "*Vielen dank*, both of you. We're excited to have them here."

Rebecca climbed back onto the wagon seat. Jacob settled beside her and took up the reins. Waving and exclaiming their appreciation, the Schrock family returned to their home.

Full darkness was upon them as Jacob directed the horse back to Caleb's farm. "The bee yard is going to seem so empty now," he ventured.

"*Ja*, but it's a job well done." Rebecca repinned her *kapp*, which had come loose under the bee veil. "It's been *gut* to get this business started. Who knows? Maybe some other church members will start keeping hives of their own."

"One thing is certain—this project has been a lot more successful than I thought it would. We work better together than against each other," teased Jacob. "When I first arrived, I thought you were going to push me into the compost pile sometimes."

"I wanted to," she admitted, smiling at the memory. "But I guess you turned out okay." More than okay, she thought. She'd warmed up to Jacob in ways she hadn't expected. He was a fine business partner, yes. But somehow, over the last few weeks, he had become a good friend as well.

She wasn't analytical by nature. She simply accepted things as they came. And if Jacob had turned into a comfortable work associate, she accepted that and looked no further.

She was glad her life was settling back into a normal, pleasant routine.

Jacob overslept the next morning. When he walked, blinking and yawning, into the kitchen, he found Rebecca cooking breakfast.

"Where's Caleb?" he asked, wiping sleep from his eyes.

"Getting the mail. He'll be back in a few minutes." She checked on something in the oven and continued stirring scrambled eggs in a pan.

She looked tidy and neat in her dark green dress and black apron. Her white *kapp* caught a shaft of morning sunlight and made her look more beautiful than usual. He tried not to watch her too obviously, though he found himself admiring her.

Caleb came in shortly thereafter, carrying a bundle of envelopes. *"Guder mariye, guder mariye,"* he said in a rumbling tone. "Mail for everyone today. Jacob, these are yours. Rebecca, one for you. And I got a letter from my *schwester*."

Jacob glanced through his mail—two bills and a letter from a friend back in Ohio—and set them aside as Rebecca began putting dishes on the table.

After the silent blessing, Caleb asked, "What's on the agenda today?"

"Gardening," replied Rebecca promptly. "I need to get some weeding done."

"And pond-digging," added Jacob. "I'm going to be working on the new water course."

"I never would have thought about damming that small drainage, but I agree it will be *gut* to have another pond," commented Caleb.

"And this afternoon I'm going to plan the food I'm bringing to tomorrow's barn raising," continued Rebecca. "I thought I'd bring a couple of hash brown casseroles—those are always popular—and if I make them tonight and bake them early tomorrow morning, they'll stay hot in the insulated carriers."

"Rebecca makes the most mouthwatering hash brown casserole," Caleb said to him. "Wait until you taste it."

"Hopefully they won't get snapped up too quick tomorrow," he remarked. He was looking forward to the work party, which always brought out a masculine camaraderie he enjoyed. "Whose barn are we building, by the way?"

"Oliver Yoder's," replied Caleb. "No relation to the Yoder family that owns the mercantile in town. Oliver and Beth Yoder moved out here last fall and we built them a house, but they're desperately in need of a barn. They're nice folks. You'll like them."

"I haven't met anyone out here yet that I *haven't* liked." Jacob winked at the older man. "Have I thanked you lately for leaving me the farm?" He was pleased to hear his uncle's chuckle.

Caleb was in charge of dishes this morning since Rebecca had made breakfast, so after the meal Jacob dropped his mail in his bedroom and grabbed his work gloves. He emerged from the outside kitchen door to see Rebecca stopped on the path halfway to her cabin. She had her head bent as she read the letter that had arrived in the morning mail.

Something about her posture alarmed him. He walked up behind her. "Everything *oll recht*?"

"What?" She whirled, her eyes wide and startled. "Sorry, I didn't hear you. No, everything's not *oll recht*," she added, tears suddenly springing to her eyes.

In the weeks since meeting her, he had never seen Rebecca lose control of her emotions. The letter must contain bad news indeed.

"Bad news?" he asked.

"*Nein!* Infuriating news. I can't believe it!" Her voice rose and she waved the letter around.

"Can't believe what?"

"I can't believe what my *mamm* wrote to me. You know who is planning on coming to visit me here? Jeremiah, that's who. The man who dumped me at the altar now apparently has had a change of heart and wants to court me!" She whirled and stamped away.

He followed her as she stepped onto the small porch of her cabin. "Can you write and tell your *mamm* that you don't want him to come?"

"What *gut* would it do?" She yanked open the cabin door and went inside.

After a moment's hesitation, he followed. He'd never seen the inside of her cabin, and he glanced around to take in the clean lines, comfortable furnishings, generous bookshelves and airy curtains. He watched as she slammed the letter down on the plain pine table, crossed her arms and glowered at the small wood cookstove tucked in a corner.

He spoke carefully. "Start over. Your *mamm* said your former betrothed is coming to Montana. How did he know you were here? Did she tell him?"

She transferred her glare to him, though he knew he was merely a convenient target. "I can only imagine she did. Argh! Why does she feel the need to interfere with my love life? Can't she understand I'd rather stay single forever than marry someone who didn't think I was *gut* enough five years ago?"

He felt a twinge of sympathy. Rebecca seemed to get along with her family well enough, but this degree of personal interference from her mother rose to another level.

"Okay, stop and think rationally for a moment," he suggested. Uninvited, he seated himself at the small kitchen table. "Can you write to your *mamm* and tell this Jeremiah fellow not to come?"

"I wish it were that simple. I suspect Jeremiah is curious about the Montana community and is thinking perhaps he'd want to settle out here. Why couldn't he have stayed in the *Englisch* world?"

"You don't know why he returned?"

"*Nein.* We haven't been in touch since he broke up with me. Even his insults were secondhand." This last statement was made with a touch of wry humor.

Jacob sensed the worst was over. "Well, I have an idea on how you might be able to salvage this situation and put him off, but I'm not sure you're going to want to hear it."

"At this point, I'm willing to hear anything. The last thing I want is for Jeremiah to show up on my doorstep."

"*Oll recht.* What do you think of this? Write back to your *mamm* and tell her you're already being courted."

"*Ja* sure, like she'd believe *that,*" answered Rebecca with deep sarcasm.

"Seriously. Tell her you and I are courting."

Startled, she stared at him. "You and I?"

"Ja."

Looking boneless, she dropped into a chair opposite from him. "Jacob, where did this come from?"

He gestured at the letter. "You need some way to get your mother off your back. What better way than to tell her your affections are already engaged elsewhere?"

She snorted with derision, which at any other time he might consider insulting. Instead, he was amused.

"Ja," she said. "It would certainly solve the immediate issue. But what happens when November comes and goes and no wedding occurs?"

"You can cross that bridge when you come to it. We could develop a convenient case of irreconcilable differences, long before your family travels out here for a wedding."

She drummed her fingers on the table, staring into the distance, then nodded. "Okay. Let me write something out and then let you read it before I send. That way you're not getting into something too deep."

"Ja gut." He stood up. "I'm heading to the new pond site. Are you going to write the letter now or later?"

"Later, I suppose. I want to think on what I'm going to say."

He nodded and made his way toward the door. But her voice stopped him.

"Jacob?"

"Ja?" He turned. She suddenly looked very vulnerable, sitting alone at the little kitchen table in her small cabin.

"Danke," she said. "Even if this doesn't work, I appreciate you wanting to help."

He smiled and nodded, then touched the brim of his hat and walked out the door.

Heading for the pond site, he wondered what impulse caused him to make such an offer. It certainly seemed off-the-cuff and impetuous.

Or was it?

Sometimes things in his life seemed prompted by none other than *Gott*. Caleb's offer to make him the heir to this farm was the biggest example. But since coming out here and realizing he was in a much better position to marry and have a family, Jacob had been wondering when he would meet the right woman. Rebecca hadn't been a candidate at first; her hostility seemed too deep to overcome. But now…

Maybe his impromptu offer of pretend courtship was sent from *Gott*. How else could he have blurted out such an outrageous suggestion?

Since their work with the hive rentals, their relationship had shifted and he had come to admire her. Her strength of character matched her strength of features, and he had come to appreciate both. She was well-liked in the community by people who had known her longer than he had, which indicated a good nature.

But that nagging question remained—why *hadn't* she married after all these years in Montana? Neither she nor Caleb, nor anyone else, had ever hinted at so much as an infatuation on her part. Did she have such a deep fear of marriage? Did she truly mean to remain single all her life? It seemed a lonely existence to Jacob.

He seized a shovel and tackled the widening area of the pond location, thinking it over.

Rebecca was a tough nut to crack. He wasn't used to dealing with such independent women.

He smiled as he deepened the pond site with the shovel. Independent, yes. Difficult, yes. Smart, opinionated, intriguing, complex…yes.

What a woman.

Okay, so she would tell her family she was being courted. November, after the harvest season, was the time most Amish couples got married. He suspected she would string the fictional arrangement along—by letter—until about October, which was about the time she would have to end the courtship lest her parents actually start planning the wedding.

So as he figured it, he had until October to convince her to change their fictional courtship to a real one.

But how?

He could use some advice, and Caleb knew her better than anyone, at least here in Montana. Courtship was something new for him, and he wasn't entirely sure how to break through Rebecca's walls and convince her he wasn't anything like the cad Jeremiah, who had hurt her so deeply.

Suddenly he paused in his work, feeling a shaft of

uncertainty flow through him. Was he himself worthy of someone like Rebecca? How did she view him—as a decent man or a nuisance? It had certainly been the latter when they first met.

He resumed his work. Yes, he would talk to Caleb and ask for his uncle's help in the matter.

Chapter Thirteen

Courtship? With Jacob?

Even fictional, the notion of being courted by Jacob made Rebecca nervous. Sitting alone in her cabin after he had left, she wondered why.

It took a few moments to recognize the emotion for what it was: fear. She was frightened of courtship, frightened of marriage, frightened of making a lifelong mistake like her poor friend Leah had done.

Why couldn't her mother and aunt understand that? There had been times in the past five years she had broken into a cold sweat at the thought of what might have happened if she and Jeremiah had gone through with their vows, and she never failed to thank *Gott* for helping her avoid that trap.

Jacob might wonder why she hadn't married in the five years she'd been in Montana, but the truth was she wouldn't allow anyone to court her. She had worked hard to develop an independent life, and was content to continue as she was.

And yet…she had to admit that she'd reached an age where she recognized independence might not be enough. The *Englisch* had a term for it: her biological clock. She had always envisioned herself with *kinner*, and *kinner* weren't possible without a *hutband* first.

And to be fair, every other marriage she knew was a happy one. Her parents had a happy marriage. So did her aunts and uncles, and her older brothers and sisters. Marrying someone within the church practically guaranteed at least a contented union. Leah's outright incompatibility with her *hutband* was unusual.

And what left a bitter taste in Rebecca's mouth about her friend's situation was that Leah would likely have figured this out before the wedding had the busybody older women in the church just left her alone. Instead, they had pushed the match—just as they pushed Jeremiah on her—and now Leah was irrevocably bound to a man she didn't much like.

That terrified Rebecca. What if the same thing happened to her? Maybe her standards were too high, but she didn't want to settle for an incompatible match just so she could have *kinner* one day.

She picked up the letter from her mother and scanned the tidy handwriting. Sighing, she fetched a piece of paper and a pen, and began drafting a reply. She intended to show it to Jacob so he could suggest any changes.

She spun a vague tale of the growing admiration she felt for Caleb's heir after their initial period of conflict, and how they worked together with the bees building up the hive rental business. She prevaricated that while she didn't know what the future would bring, she was certain it didn't include Jeremiah, so she urged her mother with all speed to discourage him from traveling to Montana.

Half an hour later, she folded the sheet, and headed out to the new pond location. Jacob was digging his shovel into the soil as she approached.

"Will you read this over when you have a moment?" she asked him. "No rush. It's just a draft of how I'm going to phrase things to my *mamm*. You're welcome to make any changes to it. It's just fiction, after all."

"Danke." He eyed her. "Are you *oll recht*?"

"Ja." She passed a hand over her face in a gesture of weariness. "Just thinking about my friend Leah, and how she might have discovered in time that she and her *hutband* were not compatible if she hadn't been swept away by the matchmaking ladies in our church. It's by the grace of *Gott* Jeremiah and I never went through with it. Anyway, make whatever changes you like on that, and I'll include them when I write back to *Mamm*."

"Ja gut." He pocketed the folded sheet.

Rebecca walked back to the garden and fetched a crate to sit on from the small open-sided shed, where she stored gardening tools. Then she picked a bed and settled down to weed.

She liked weeding. It was soothing and easy and useful. It was also her prayer time, a time she could talk to *Gott* on easy terms, and be more open to listening to His response.

So she asked for guidance on her future. Jacob's off-the-cuff offer of convenient courtship might have solved the temporary issue of keeping Jeremiah from showing up unannounced, but it wasn't a real courtship. November would come and go, and she wouldn't be any more married than she was now.

And for the first time, she wondered if she wanted that to change.

"Lead me, *Gott,*" she whispered. If there was a man out there meant for her, she hoped *Gott* would let her know.

But hours later, when it was time for lunch, she was no closer to an answer.

Caleb rang the triangular dinner bell to summon them for the midday meal. Rebecca dusted off her hands and followed Jacob as she made her way to the kitchen.

After the blessing on the food, Jacob looked at her. "The letter reads fine," he said. "I have nothing else to add." He slid the folded-up sheet of paper across the table to her.

"Ja gut. Danke," she replied, then speared a potato. She slipped the paper into her pocket.

"Letter?" asked Caleb with his mouth full.

Rebecca hesitated a moment, then told Caleb the full story. "I gave Jacob the rough outline of what I was going to write back to my mother," she concluded, "so he could change anything he wanted."

"A pretend courtship, eh?" The older man's eyes twinkled. "Think it will work?"

"All I want is to keep Jeremiah from showing up on my doorstep," retorted Rebecca. "I'm grateful Jacob came up with the idea. I don't know what else I could do to keep Jeremiah from coming out here."

"Do you think your *mamm* has anything to do with Jeremiah wanting to travel to Montana?" inquired Caleb.

"That's my suspicion, *ja*. How else would he know where I am?" said Rebecca. "I know *Mamm* thinks everyone is happier when they're married. I love my *mutter*, but I wish she would just *stop*." Rebecca could hear the frustration in her own voice.

Caleb patted her hand, then resumed his meal. "Let it rest in *Gott*'s hands," he advised. "The Lord works in mysterious ways."

After lunch, Jacob trooped out to resume work on his project by the pond. Rebecca gathered dishes and prepared to clean the kitchen, since Caleb had cooked the meal.

"*Liebling*, you still seem upset," Caleb observed gently, lingering as she heated water for washing.

She felt unwanted tears prickle her eyes. "*Ja*, I am," she replied. "Here I am, fifteen hundred miles away from my family, yet my *mamm* can still reach out and disturb my peace of mind. It's a gift, Caleb," she ended sarcastically.

"Hmm. But if you tell your *mamm* you and Jacob are courting, won't she make plans to come out for a wedding in November?"

"Not if I tell her the courtship has ended in October. That was Jacob's idea." She added soap to the dishpan. "But it irks me that I need to resort to subterfuge just to get my family to stop focusing on my marital status."

"Well, who knows what *Gott* has in store for you. I'm just glad Jacob was able to step in and offer a temporary solution."

"*Ja*, me, too. But I don't like lying."

"Someday you may not have to." Caleb glanced at the

clock over the kitchen sink. "I'm off to meet Ephraim in town for coffee. I'll be back in a couple hours."

The older man planted a kiss on her cheek and walked out of the kitchen. She stared after him. What did he mean? And why did she suddenly have an ominous feeling in her gut?

After the lunch dishes were washed, she pulled together the ingredients for hash brown casserole and began to assemble the dish. Her mind flip-flopped all over the place, battered by the emotions she had long thought she'd left behind.

Yet she was confident Jacob's ruse of courting her would work. Knowing her mother as she did, she had no doubt word would spread like wildfire all over her hometown that her headstrong youngest daughter was getting married at last. Jeremiah would just have to find some other woman to court.

And when the inevitable follow-up letter arrived—long before November's traditional wedding month—to say the courtship had ended…well, her *mamm* would be disappointed, but at least Jeremiah wouldn't be inclined to travel to Montana, either.

She finished assembling the three hash brown casseroles and slid them into the icebox until the following morning. Then she departed for her cabin to finish writing the letter to her mother.

"So what is a courting man supposed to do?" inquired Jacob in a light voice as he and Rebecca worked together to do the evening chores.

"I have no idea," she replied. "It's been years since I courted. And the last time I tried it, it ended in disaster."

"I've never tried it myself," he mused, grunting a bit as he speared some hay and pitched it into a cart. "I'd be at a loss if this was a real-life situation."

Rebecca straddled the milking stool, slid a bucket under one of the cows and began zinging milk into the pail. "I'm trying not to be angry with my *mamm*," she said, her voice somewhat muffled by the cow's flank.

"I never appreciated how invasive matchmaking could be," he agreed. "I'm grateful no one ever tried it on me." He paused. "Except, possibly, Caleb."

She gave a snort of laughter. "*Ja*, he tried that on me, too. Caleb is a dear, though. I can't be angry with him for trying to push us together."

"It must be hard, being his age and not having any family nearby. No wife, no *kinner*."

"I'm kind of surprised he left his extended family behind to move to Montana," agreed Rebecca. "He left behind his entire support system."

"He has an adventurous streak in him. That's the only thing I can think of."

"*Ja*, I understand that." She kept up with the milking, her movements quick and efficient. "I did the same thing. But in my case, it was a matter of escape."

"Have you been home to Indiana to visit since moving out here?"

"*Ja*, once or twice. *Mamm* never stops remarking about my single state, and it's difficult seeing my friend Leah in her unhappy marriage. Frankly, it's a relief to come back here, where everything seems simpler."

"Does your *mamm* take any responsibility for Leah's marriage?"

"I don't know." Milk zinged into the metal pail. "I've never asked her. The Bible instructs us to honor our *vader und mutter*, and asking seems disrespectful."

They did the chores by rote, and Jacob was pleased to hear Rebecca making more small talk as they worked to get the chickens, cows and horses ready for the night.

Jacob was just about to close the barn door behind the last horse when a movement caught his eye.

The sun had set but dusk lingered on. As he watched, a bear ambled out of the shadows of the trees beyond the bee yard. He caught his breath.

Evidently noticing his reaction, Rebecca silently stepped to his side. When she saw the bear, she stiffened and gasped.

"*Nein*, don't," he ordered, grasping her arm as she tensed. He was concerned she would race toward the bruin to chase it off. "See what happens. Let's see if the fence holds."

"But if it doesn't, he'll do a lot of damage," she whispered in a panicky voice, her eyes as wide as saucers.

"We'll have plenty of time to get there if he starts to destroy the fence. Wait and see."

"Then at least let's slip over there, by that shed. We'll be closer." The bee yard was a distance from the barn.

"Ja gut." He fastened the barn door behind them, took her hand and slipped toward the shed. He peeked around the corner and motioned for Rebecca to follow.

The bear lingered outside the fence of the bee yard, swaying back and forth as it contemplated how to breach the defenses. At one point, it rose on its hind legs and rested its front paws on the deer netting, which sagged a bit under the weight but looked nowhere ready to buckle. Then the bear dropped back to the ground and began walking around the fence, sniffing and investigating.

Jacob felt rather than saw Rebecca relax as she witnessed the strength of the fence and the bruin's inability to find a way in.

"I think having the flexibility of the deer netting is a benefit," he murmured to her. "It bends with the weight of the bear but doesn't break, and he can't climb anything that saggy."

"Danke, Gott," she breathed, staring at the animal.

Jacob had never really seen a bear up close, and he found himself fascinated by the animal. Its head was broad with a narrow muzzle, and he could see the large hinged jaw. Its paws were large, clawed and powerful.

"No wonder they can rip a hive to pieces," he murmured in Rebecca's ear. "Look at those paws. I'd hate to be on the receiving end."

"Bears are surprisingly dexterous, too," she replied in a low voice. "I've heard stories of them opening car doors and even jar lids. By comparison, getting into a hive is easy for them, starting with just knocking them over."

"Just sheer strength," he muttered. "They're incredibly strong animals. That's why I didn't want you running after it. If he'd turned on you, you wouldn't have had a chance."

"I know that now." She sighed. "Don't worry, I'm not about to run after it this time."

"Unless it breaks through the fence and starts on a hive." He grinned at her in the gloom of dusk. "In which case I'm going to have to hold you back."

"It won't be necessary. Look." She pointed.

Jacob saw that the bear, having encircled the entire bee yard, had given up and was wandering back into the woods. He breathed a sigh of relief, which was echoed by Rebecca.

"Danke, Gott," he said, repeating her earlier prayer.

"Ja." She straightened up from her tense half crouch. "I've been in Montana five years now, and have never once seen a bear before this one decided to show up."

"I hope this one doesn't keep hanging around. It makes me nervous about leaving the livestock out at night, even during the warm summer months," remarked Jacob. He started walking back toward the barn, feeling troubled and unsettled.

"There's a fellow on the settlement named Benjamin Troyer who breeds Great Pyrenees guard dogs. Maybe we should get a couple of them."

"That's a *gut* idea!" He brightened. "I've met Benjamin. Do you think he'll be at the barn raising tomorrow? I could talk to him about getting some dogs."

"*Ja*, I'm sure he'll be there. I can't put a dog in the bee yard, though, so I'm grateful the fence held."

"You know…" Jacob spun around and looked at the bee yard, just visible in the darkening evening. He gestured. "What we might be able to do is expand the pasture fence to include the bee yard. We couldn't do that earlier because we couldn't risk cows or horses walking right among the hives. But since the yard is now stoutly fenced, we could expand the pasture for the animals to graze. That way, if we get guard dogs, they can protect the bee yard as well, like an island within the pasture."

"Jacob, that's a *gut* idea!" He saw a flash of teeth in the dark as she smiled at him. "And I will sleep better at night!"

"I will, too." He walked beside her toward the house. "Frankly, it's a relief to think of a solution."

"Men seem to be very solution-oriented," she observed, striding beside him.

"Ja," he replied. "I guess that's how *Gott* made us. You were worried about the bees. I found a solution. I like *doing* things."

He heard her give a faint gasp. He turned and, in the gloaming, saw a startled look on her face. She stopped walking.

He stopped, too. "What's wrong?"

"Nothing." She started walking again. "Just remembering something my *grossmammi* told me many years ago."

He shrugged and kept pace with her. It was yet another example of Rebecca's enigmatic personality. She was like a many-layered puzzle, something he had to figure out piece by piece. He found himself enjoying the challenge.

Chapter Fourteen

After a restless night's sleep, Rebecca rose early to bake the hash brown casseroles she'd made the day before. The baking took two hours, so she needed to get an early start. She found herself hoping her friend Eva Hostetler would be at the barn raising. She could use some feminine insight right about now.

Her *grossmammi*'s words had haunted her throughout the night. Jacob's idea to keep her hives safe by getting guard dogs certainly could be due to his own vested interest, now that he had a stake in hive rentals. But somehow, it seemed more than that. Or was she reading too much into the situation?

Having avoided any emotional entanglements for the past five years, she didn't know. That's why she hoped for a few private minutes with Eva, so she could reap the other woman's guidance and experience.

While the food was baking, she did the usual barn chores, then came back into the kitchen with buckets of milk in hand to find Caleb making breakfast. Jacob sat at the kitchen table, sipping coffee.

"Guder mariye," Caleb greeted. "And how is my nephew's betrothed this morning?"

"Guder mariye," she returned, and rolled her eyes in Jacob's direction. "Just the same as always. Caleb, I beg you, don't spread rumors at the barn raising today. I don't want to have to explain why I was metaphorically left at the altar again."

"Don't worry, I won't say a word." The older man winked, then returned to the bacon he was frying. "Though it seems like a waste of a perfectly *gut* opportunity."

"What, spreading false gossip?" teased Jacob.

"*Nein*, the chance to actually court."

"Jacob and I agreed last night we didn't have the faintest idea how to go about it, and since it's a moot point, what difference does it make?" Rebecca set about straining the milk into clean jars, then set them in the icebox to cool down. "But I've found people are far more inclined to bend their ears toward gossip than the truth, so I don't want any rumors to get started."

"You have my promise." Caleb smiled.

Rebecca knew Caleb was a man of his word, but some uneasiness still lingered. She had a suspicion her mentor had something up his sleeve.

After the morning meal, things got busy. Rebecca washed the breakfast dishes and then she tucked the hash brown casseroles into insulated containers. Caleb and Jacob gathered up the tools they would need for the barn raising. While Caleb didn't engage in much of the actual construction at his age, he often oversaw the younger boys, guiding and teaching them some of the simpler carpentry tasks.

Jacob hitched the horse to the wagon. Caleb climbed up into the front seat next to Jacob, and Rebecca rode on the tailgate of the wagon, the basket of food tucked securely behind her.

The day was bright and promised to be warm later. Rebecca sniffed the fresh morning air. She saw other wagons heading toward the work party, as well as people walking alongside the road. There was a carnival atmosphere to the thickening stream of people all heading toward a common goal. She waved and called greetings.

The farm where the barn was to be raised was thick with church members bustling around. Rebecca hopped off the back of the wagon and took the basket of food.

"Take the tools and get going," Caleb told Jacob. "I'll take care of the horse and wagon. See that group over there? Adam Chupp is the foreman of this project, and he has the plans. He'll explain your part."

"Ja gut." Jacob shouldered his tool belt, grabbed two toolboxes and departed.

"I'll be with the rest of the women," Rebecca told Caleb. He nodded and smiled, then drove the wagon away to unhitch the horse.

Rebecca greeted the various matrons as the women worked to unpack hampers and set up tables. She kept a special eye out for Eva Hostetler, but her friend had not arrived yet.

When she finally saw the Hostetler family drive up in their wagon, she felt a sense of relief. She realized how much she was looking forward to asking Eva's advice.

It took several minutes for the other family to unhitch and unload. Soon, Eva came along, shepherding her two older children. A toddler clutched her skirt and she carried the youngest baby on one arm and a hamper with the other. Rebecca walked over to meet her.

"Jacob, there's Lucas, over with the rest of the boys." Eva pointed. "You can go join them, *ja*?"

"Ja," said her oldest boy, who shared a first name with Caleb's nephew. He darted off.

Rebecca smiled as she watched the boy dash away. "He looks like he's eager to learn carpentry," she said to Eva.

"He is, though how much he learns when he has Lucas to play with is questionable. *Danke*," she added, as Rebecca relieved her of the hamper. "And I have some *gut* news for you."

"What kind of *gut* news?" Rebecca smiled at the baby and chucked him under the chin.

"I may have found a job for you, and a place to live."

Rebecca stopped in her tracks. So much had happened in the last couple of months that she'd forgotten Eva wasn't up on the latest developments. "Oh..."

Eva stopped, too. "Unless things have improved?" she inquired. "And you no longer need to find a place to live?"

"*Ja*, that's it exactly." Relieved, Rebecca started walking again. "I have a lot to tell you, it seems."

"After lunch, we'll find a quiet spot and have a *gut* chat. We'll be too busy before then."

She was right. Rebecca got caught up in spreading out food, setting up makeshift tables and bringing drinks to the hardworking carpenters as the structure took shape under their skilled hands.

At noon, the men broke for lunch, then went right back to work. The women and children ate afterward, lingering over their food. Over the cadence of banging hammers, Rebecca heard the pleasant hum of chatter and feminine laughter, and the shrieking of children playing, and realized afresh how much she loved the church camaraderie.

Eva's baby had fallen asleep. She laid him on a blanket under a tree and went to help clean up the lunch mess. Then, while the rest of the women fell to quilting or sewing, she and Eva sat on the blanket with the sleeping baby and caught up with each other.

"First, what situation did you think I might like?" inquired Rebecca, resting her back against the tree.

"Ruby Lapp's sewing business is expanding," replied Eva. "She's too busy to keep up with her big garden, and wouldn't mind having something of a live-in companion to help with the gardening and sewing. She has a little guesthouse where you could live. There would be room for the bees on her property. But you said you don't need it now?"

Rebecca liked Ruby, an older widow. But she shook her head. "Jacob and I have come to an understanding." She grinned. "He wanted my bees and didn't know we were a package deal."

"Are you getting along better these days?"

"*Ja.* There are times I still want to strangle him.

But we started a small business a while ago—renting out hives."

"I thought I saw hives on other farms! I didn't know they were yours."

"*Ja*, people have wanted hives for some time, but it's a two-person job. I can't move them on my own. Anyway, we've had to learn to work together because of that, so it's better now between us. In fact..." To her annoyance, she felt her face heat up. "In fact, I wouldn't mind some advice."

"*Ja* sure. What's the matter?"

Knowing Eva wasn't a gossip, Rebecca explained the circumstances under which she and Jacob had entered a false courtship. "But here's the thing," she concluded. "*I* know it's fake. *He* knows it's fake. But he's doing things that *don't* seem fake, if you know what I mean."

"What kind of things?"

"Like working hard to build a fence around the bee yard to keep a pesky bear away. That was the first thing I noticed. My *grossmammi* once told me that men show affection not by words, but by actions. My concern is Jacob's fake courtship may not be as fake on his end as I hope it is."

"And you don't want him to court you?" Eva's expression was sympathetic.

"Nein." Troubled, Rebecca plucked a dandelion leaf and absently tore it to pieces. *"Nein."*

"Are you sure?" persisted Eva with a faint smile. "Because sometimes it seems the harder one protests, the more it's hiding something. Forgive me if I'm wrong, but it seems you like Jacob well enough, but perhaps you're just gun-shy about getting married."

"You always were a wise woman, Eva." Rebecca made a rueful expression. "Maybe that's the case. We seem to get along now, but it's marriage I'm scared of." Eva knew about her friend Leah's situation. "Marriage is forever. What if I make a mistake?"

"That's what courtship is for. Real courtship, that is. Did your friend Leah truly have a chance to be courted by her *hutband*, or were they just sort of pushed together?"

"Pushed, I guess. Just like I was with Jeremiah."

"But you're not being pushed toward Jacob," Eva replied. "I mean, *ja*, this is sort of a courtship of convenience, but if it should turn into something real, would that be such a bad thing?"

Rebecca was silent, staring off at the group of men working on the barn structure. The background sound of hammers and saws was soothing. It wasn't hard to pick out Jacob from the group—she seemed to have a knack for spotting him.

"I don't know," she finally replied.

"Then that's what you need to figure out," said Eva. At that moment, her infant son woke up and began crying, and the matron picked him up to soothe him. "But one thing is certain. *Gott* has a special someone in mind for you. Don't push him away in sheer stubbornness."

"I like work parties," Jacob remarked as he banged a nail. "They always seem to bring out the best in people."

"I agree," said his carpentry partner for the day, a

man named Daniel Hostetler. "It's a nice break from regular work, too. How's the farm coming along?"

"It's doing well. I've got two big projects I'm working on this summer—a no-till garden and a pond for capturing runoff. And I'm learning about beekeeping, too."

"Rebecca is remarkable with bees," Daniel replied as he banged vigorously on a nail.

"We've been having some trouble with a visiting bear," said Jacob. "Rebecca actually chased it away from the hives a while ago, so we hastily put up a fence. So far it's holding, but she's worried it may breach the defenses. She said Benjamin Troyer breeds Great Pyrenees dogs, and that I might consider looking into them. I'm sure I've met Benjamin, but I'm still getting people straight."

"*Ja*, Benjamin's dogs are always in demand." Daniel chuckled. "In fact, he has a kind of dog-rental service in which he'll place a pair of dogs with your livestock on a month-to-month basis. That way you can test-run them, so to speak."

"Is he here today?"

"Ja." Daniel scanned the group of men working on the barn, then pointed. "That's him in the green shirt."

"Danke." Jacob made sure to memorize the man's features. "I'll catch up with him later and ask about them. It will make Rebecca happy to know her hives are protected."

"Ah, that's what I thought."

Startled, Jacob glanced at Daniel, who had a big smile on his face. "What do you mean?"

"I mean, I was wondering if Rebecca was more to you than just a farm hand. Sounds like she might be something more, if you're going out of your way to do things that will make her happy."

"Ha." The other man was just too discerning, but Jacob didn't deny his words. "I can assure you, it's one-sided. She had a bad experience back in Indiana before moving out here to help Caleb, and she's been wary of marriage ever since. I might be interested in courting her, but I don't think she'll have it."

"But a couple of dogs to guard her beehives might be a *gut* start."

"Ja." Jacob grinned at the other man. "That was my thought, too."

"Talk to Benjamin. He's a *gut* man, and his wife, Abigail, is friends with Rebecca."

After lunch, but before work resumed on the barn, Jacob sought out Benjamin Troyer and explained the situation.

"*Ja*, I have a male-female pair you can use," Benjamin replied. "Pyrenees work best in pairs. I heard you and Rebecca are renting out hives. That's what I do with my dogs sometimes—it gives people a chance to see what guard dogs are like, to see if they want to get a pair of their own permanently."

"Ja gut." Jacob made arrangements to pick up the dogs after he had adequately fenced the newer section of pasture that would encompass the bee yard. He found himself glowing with excitement at the thought of relaying these developments to Rebecca. He was, he realized, trying to impress her—and more importantly, trying to break down that seemingly impenetrable barrier around her heart.

At the end of the day, Jacob was tired but satisfied with his efforts. The barn still needed some work, but the hardest part was done and the structure was sound. It never failed to fill his heart with gratitude to be part of a group that could accomplish so much through co-operation.

"Ready to go home?" Caleb called out, striding toward him as he packed away his tools.

"Ja," he replied. "And I have something to discuss with both you and Rebecca on the drive home."

The older man raised his bushy eyebrows but said nothing more. Instead, he turned to go hitch up the horse.

Half an hour later, Rebecca climbed into the back of the wagon amid the food hamper and toolboxes. Jacob swung onto the wagon seat next to Caleb. Friends called out their goodbyes as Jacob clucked to the horse and they started down the road.

"So what did you want to discuss?" asked Caleb.

"Dogs." Jacob turned so Rebecca could hear the conversation. "You were right to talk to Benjamin. He has a pair of Great Pyrenees he can rent to us on a month-by-month basis."

"Danke!" exclaimed Rebecca. Her smile lit up her face. "I'll feel so much better about the hives—and about the livestock, too."

"I've never had guard dogs." Caleb looked thoughtful. "But I've heard *gut* things about them." He glanced at Jacob. "Why did you decide *now* to get dogs? Why not earlier?"

"Because the beehives weren't fenced earlier. Now

we can let the cows and horses nearby, and guard dogs will keep any bears away from everything."

"Is that the *only* reason?"

"*Ja*, of course." Jacob glanced sharply at Caleb. "What other reason could there be?"

"*Nichts.* Nothing." The older man turned his head and gazed out at the scenery.

Jacob wasn't fooled. It was clear his uncle had drawn the same conclusion as Daniel had earlier. The reason behind his desire to please Rebecca was evident to everyone but Rebecca.

But the same uneasiness lingered. It wasn't like Caleb to be sly.

He was interested in courting Rebecca, yes. But it had to be on her terms, no one else's. Not his, not Caleb's, not her mother's. He was a patient man. He could wait.

He glanced unobtrusively at Rebecca. She, too, was watching the passing scenery, and there was a half smile on her face. He found himself looking forward to those smiles. It made everything worthwhile.

Rebecca's strong personality appealed to him. Other women paled in comparison as a result. She was nobody's fool and nobody's doormat. If, *Gott* willing, they would one day be joined in marriage, there would be times they would butt heads, but he preferred that over the alternative.

He suspected that being in her late twenties had a lot to do with her temperament. Most Amish women married much younger, but being single until now had developed Rebecca's character and disposition. Perhaps other men were intimidated by her.

But not him. He looked forward to seeing her daily, to working with her, even to clashing with her.

"We can't do anything tomorrow since it's Sunday," he said out loud, "but let's work on expanding the pasture fencing on Monday. The sooner we get it done, the sooner we can get the guard dogs, and the sooner we can stop worrying about the bear."

"Ja gut," she replied. Then she laughed. "Do guard dogs fit in with your vision of permaculture?"

"Absolutely," he replied. "In fact, the more I think about it, the more pleased I am. I know these dogs are just on loan, but if they work out, I may talk to Benjamin about either purchasing them or getting a permanent pair from him. I think we might be able to have the chickens go free-range, for example, if there are dogs around to keep the predators away."

She looked startled, then pleased. "Imagine that!"

"We may have to reinforce the pasture fences with chicken wire to keep the chickens from slipping through," he said thoughtfully, thinking through the scenario. "But free-range chickens are healthier than cooped-up chickens, even with the use of chicken tractors. So, *ja*, I think these dogs will be an excellent addition to a permaculture farm."

"I'm impressed," admitted Caleb. "I had my doubts when you first started talking about all this permaculture stuff, but it does seem to have some merit."

"The whole idea is to make less work, not more," replied Jacob. "*Ja*, it's more work in the beginning, like any project. But I hope to do justice to what you've accomplished here, Uncle Caleb."

"What I've accomplished here *with Rebecca*," replied Caleb meaningfully. "She was just as instrumental as I was in making it productive. Possibly more, since she has the stronger back. This farm would be nothing without her."

From the corner of his eye, Jacob saw Rebecca smile with fondness at the older man. "That's why I love this property as much as you do," she said.

The older man chuckled. "*Ja gut.* Who knows what may happen, then?"

Once again a shadow of concern pierced Jacob's frame of mind. He couldn't shake the feeling that Caleb was planning something.

But he refused to let any concerns spoil the sweet victory of the day. Not only had he made a good impression with the other men in the church community with his carpentry skills, but he'd also solved the issue of the visiting bear in a method that pleased Rebecca.

As he turned the horse up the driveway toward home, he decided life was good.

Chapter Fifteen

"Do you get the feeling," said Rebecca to Jacob as she helped unroll a bundle of fencing, "that Caleb is planning some sort of chicanery?"

Monday morning was bright and sunny, and they had made good progress on the new pasture fencing as they prepared to take possession of the pair of rental guard dogs.

Jacob turned from where he was working to attach the fencing to the T-posts. *"Ja!"* he exclaimed. "I thought it was just me!"

"At breakfast this morning, when he said he had an errand to do in town, I got a distinct impression he was being evasive for some reason." She frowned. "That's not like him."

"Yet he seemed pleased somehow," agreed Jacob. "His eyes were all twinkly, like he was keeping a happy secret."

"I love that man to pieces, but it's not like him to act like this."

"Well, there's not much we can do about it." With deft movements, Jacob snipped a piece of thin wire and used it to fasten the fence to the post. "Meanwhile, if we keep making the progress we are, I don't see why we can't get the dogs later this week."

"Then we should start making rounds of the rental hives and checking to make sure they're all doing well," she said. "We should start with the first hives we rented, and work our way down the list."

"Ja gut."

The morning sped by until Rebecca realized it was almost lunchtime. "Caleb said he'd be back by lunchtime, so I'll go get the meal started."

"And I'll keep working on the fence. Ring the dinner bell when you need me."

Rebecca returned to the house and began pulling together lunch.

A smile lingered on her face as she assembled a sandwich bar. She found she enjoyed working with Jacob. When they had a common goal—such as expanding the pasture around the bee yard and getting guard dogs—she forgot she ever had a quarrel with him. He was easy to talk to and—not incidentally—easy on the eyes, too.

She heard the clip-clop of hooves as Caleb returned from his trip to town. Through the kitchen window, she saw him direct the buggy toward the barn, then climb down from the driver's seat and unhitch the horse. Within a few minutes, he came in through the outside kitchen door.

"Guten tag," she greeted him. "What news from town?"

"Nichts," he responded, hanging his straw hat on a peg by the door. "But I did see Eva Hostetler. She says hello." He placed a thick envelope on the kitchen counter, washed his hands and began setting the table.

Rebecca rang the dinner bell to summon Jacob, and shortly thereafter they gathered in silent prayer before the food.

"So what was your errand about?" inquired Jacob with his mouth full.

"I'll tell you after we finish eating," replied Caleb, spreading mustard on his bread. "How's the fence coming for the new pasture?"

Rebecca raised her eyebrows at Caleb's obvious deflection of his errand. Jacob caught her eye and shrugged.

"Fine," replied Jacob. "We'll probably be able to bring in the guard dogs later this week."

The conversation continued until the meal was finished, then Caleb rose from his chair. "I have something to show the both of you." He fetched the envelope from the kitchen counter and returned to the table. "I was in town for an appointment with my attorney. There's a copy for each of us."

"A copy of what? What's this?" asked Jacob, taking the documents Caleb handed him.

"*Ja*, what is this?" Rebecca took her own set of documents and scanned the header, which read Last Will and Testament.

"I altered my will," explained Caleb. He smiled a beatific smile. "There is now a codicil for inheriting the farm. I'm leaving it to you both, but on one condition."

Rebecca felt a chill run through her. "Condition?"

"*Ja*, condition. I love you both and can't decide between the two of you, so the best solution is to join forces. You and Jacob must marry to inherit the farm. If you won't, then I'll sell the farm to someone else. There are always young people wanting to settle in Montana."

"I won't!" Furious anger washed through Rebecca. She exploded from her chair so fast it tipped over behind her. "I won't be pushed into marriage!"

"No one is pushing you, *liebling*..." began Caleb.

"*Ja*, you are! And you..." She whirled on Jacob. "Don't tell me you didn't have a hand in this!"

"I didn't!" he protested, a bewildered look on his face. "I had no idea this was in the works."

"Caleb, how could you do this to me?" She had to fight back violent tears of frustration. "You know how I feel about matchmaking. How could you push on me a man whose only focus is getting a farm for free?"

The older man remained maddeningly calm. "I think Jacob is more than that, *liebling*. If you only knew him better..."

"Nein!" She whirled. "All I can see is an arranged marriage. And I won't have it." She yanked open the kitchen door, and slammed it shut behind her.

The tears came as she ran to her cabin, spilling down her cheeks in a hot trail. An arranged marriage! Caleb was no better than her *mamm* and aunt. How could he think she would ever agree to something like this?

Inside her cabin, she sprawled across her bed and sobbed. All her fears welled to the surface.

She really couldn't be angry at Jacob. His protestations seemed genuine, and if Caleb was serious that he couldn't inherit the farm unless he married her, then in many ways he got the short end of the stick.

No, her anger was directed at Caleb. Her beloved mentor, the grandfatherly figure who had taken her in during her time of need, the man she had worked so closely with over the past five years—he had betrayed her. Stabbed her in the back.

It took ten minutes of hard crying to get it all out of her system. Finally, she fished a handkerchief from her pocket and mopped up her face, then turned over on her back. Staring at the ceiling, she thought things through. It was time to organize her future in a logical fashion.

Eva had said one of the older women in the community, Ruby Lapp, was looking for general help in sewing, gardening and companionship. She had a guesthouse and a space for the hives. Ruby was a pleasant woman, a fairly recent transplant from back east. Rebecca's impression was the older woman had some sort of mystery in her past, but she was easy to get along with and Rebecca liked her.

She would walk over to see Ruby tomorrow and confirm the offer. Then she would start the process of moving as soon as she could manage it. She would *not* be pushed into an unwanted marriage.

Ja, she loved this farm. But more than that, she loved her independence. She wouldn't be compelled into something that could end as disastrously as her friend Leah's marriage. She would rather end her days sewing and gardening for someone else than have her future tied irrevocably to a man she didn't pick for herself.

It would be difficult to move the remaining beehives,

but she would manage somehow. It was providential that most of the hives were now elsewhere—she only had fifteen remaining here on the farm.

She gazed up at the familiar wood beams of her little cabin and gave a dry sob. She loved this farm. She loved her little cabin. But that love did not come at the cost of her future happiness, to be yoked with a man whose intentions, she'd always suspected, were fairly mercenary. Why else would he agree to keep her on as a farm hand except that he wanted her bees?

It wasn't until the grief and anger had run its course that she had an unexpected thought: How did Jacob feel about this ultimatum? If his reaction back at the house was anything to go by, this new codicil to Caleb's will was as much a surprise to him as it was to her.

Jacob had traveled all the way from Ohio on the promise of inheriting a prime bit of farmland. Surely, he couldn't be any more pleased to be yoked with her than she was to be yoked with him.

What on earth had gotten into Caleb? Why would he risk alienating both her and Jacob—both of whom he professed to love like his own children—by requiring they marry to inherit the farm? Sourly, she wondered if her mother had put the older man up to this—except, of course, her *mamm* had never met Caleb.

She sighed and dragged herself off the bed. She had a sudden urge to sit in the bee yard—her place of refuge, the spot where her emotions had to stay in check or the bees would reflect her agitation.

Her steps dragging, she splashed her face, dried herself and went outdoors.

* * *

In the wake of Rebecca's furious departure, a sudden silence descended on the kitchen. The clock over the kitchen sink ticked loudly.

Jacob leaned back in his chair and leveled a stern look at his uncle. "That," he said, "was a mean trick to pull without any warning, for both Rebecca *and* myself."

"Maybe so, but I've been thinking about it long and hard." Caleb looked unrepentant. "I feel this is the best course of action since I love you both as the children I never had. I want you both to benefit from this farm."

"But don't you see it does the opposite?" snapped Jacob. "It yanks the carpet out from under us. I was led to believe the farm would be mine, regardless. I hope that doesn't sound greedy, because it's not meant to be. But I did uproot my entire life and move here with that basic understanding. As for Rebecca…well, you've just played into her worst fears."

Caleb raised his eyebrows. "How do you feel about Rebecca?"

"I'm inclined to say that's none of your business, but I suspect it won't do any good." Despite his annoyance, Jacob gave his uncle a rueful smile. "You have keen powers of observation. I'll admit, I'm interested in courting her."

"That's what I thought." The older man's voice was triumphant.

Jacob shook his head. "I was hoping to turn this fake courtship into something real, but I planned to go about it slowly and persuasively. Instead, you forced my hand. I can't help but be annoyed."

"She'll come around." Caleb stood to gather the lunch dishes. "I know her better than you do, and she just needs a push in the right direction."

"But that should come from inside her, not from outside. That's exactly what her mother did—push. It's like lead-training a calf, Caleb. The moment you tug on the halter, they dig in their four little hooves and won't budge when you try to pull them somewhere. It takes patient training to get them to go with you."

"It takes patient training *and* a nudge from behind," retorted Caleb with a half smile. "You've trained enough calves to know that. You're the trainer. I'm the nudger."

"She's been touchy about the issue of matchmaking since I've met her. She isn't going to go along with your new will—" Jacob tapped the papers in front of him "—just because she wants the farm. My guess is she's in her cabin making desperate alternative plans right now. I know I would be, if I were in her shoes."

"*Ja*, you could be right. But I'm confident she'll come around." Caleb put a kettle of water on the stove to heat for washing dishes. "I'm not unaware of how much I hurt her by designating you as my heir rather than her. I'm also not unaware of how much you'll benefit by having a farm of your own to support a family. Having you two get married is the perfect solution."

"Perhaps so, but that can't be forced." Jacob felt frustration well up inside him. "I was making progress with Rebecca, chipping away at her defenses with an eye toward convincing her I'm not such a bad risk as a *hutband*. Then you had to go and mess things up." With exasperated affection he added, "You're a meddling old man trying to manipulate my love life."

To his surprise, Caleb stopped fussing with the lunch dishes and dropped back into the kitchen chair he'd vacated earlier. "Jacob, let me tell you something," he said seriously. "I married Naomi when I was twenty-two. She was the love of my life. *Gott* took her from me six years ago, and I've never gotten over it." The older man's eyes were bright with moisture. "Although we couldn't have *kinner*, she was my biggest earthly blessing, and I thank *Gott* each and every day for sending me such a woman. I want the same for you and Rebecca."

Against the power of the older man's emotions, Jacob felt powerless to castigate him any further. Instead, he heaved an enormous sigh. "I loved Aunt Naomi, too," he replied gently. "But, Uncle, thanks to you, I have fences to mend. Rebecca is a stubborn woman, and whether you nudged her or not, it's going to take a lot of persuasion. And time."

The moment of sober memory was over, and Caleb's eyes twinkled once again. "Well, you have until, what, October? That's when you were going to tell her *mamm* that the courtship didn't work out so her family wouldn't travel out here expecting a wedding." He stood up. "Go on, now. Go mend some fences. I have dishes to wash."

Thus dismissed, Jacob stood up and left through the outside kitchen door, snatching his straw hat from the hat hook as he did so. He looked over at Rebecca's cabin and instinctively knew the last thing she would want at the moment was to see him.

Instead, he went to the pond site, seized a shovel and began turning his annoyed energy into labor.

The pond was taking shape. The part he was excavating made an impressive dam. Once finished, the smallish dam would create a lovely water resource in the drainage.

But a little part of him wondered if this labor of love was now an exercise in futility. Unless he could persuade Rebecca to marry him, the farm would go to someone else.

Unless he could buy it…?

Almost immediately, he rejected the thought. He certainly didn't have the money saved up, and he doubted any bank would give him a mortgage.

So he was back to square one. Inheriting the farm was supposed to be his opportunity to marry and provide for a family. Now, unless he could convince Rebecca to participate in Caleb's scheme, that hope was being snatched away from him.

He sighed and leaned on the shovel, looking around at the outbuildings, garden spaces, pasture fences and other accoutrements. Already he loved this land. He understood Rebecca's deep affection for it as well. It would hurt her to leave it. It would also hurt her to be *nudged* into marriage.

What he needed was a plan of action.

It suddenly occurred to him that Rebecca was probably unfamiliar with his changing feelings toward her. Was she even aware that his emotions had shifted from antagonism to friendliness to admiration? Perhaps honesty was the best policy.

He dug the shovel into the soil and let it stand there. Dusting off his hands, he strode toward her cabin. Hopefully, she'd had enough time to compose herself after the shock of Caleb's ultimatum. He uttered a prayer for guidance and a plea that the right words would come to him.

He needed to bridge this divide. Maybe it was the nudge he needed as well.

Chapter Sixteen

For the first time, the bees failed to calm Rebecca. She sat on the log in the bee yard, and it seemed the bees merely echoed her agitation. For some reason, it seemed a lot of bees were flying past her with a determined air. She had to resist the urge to swat them away from her as she stared at the ground, her mind churning, her midsection knotted up.

What should she do? Her brain flip-flopped this way and that. It didn't even occur to her to accept Caleb's ultimatum. Instead, her entire focus was on the logistics of moving away, coupled with the searing emotions of leaving behind the land she loved.

She stared at the ground and frowned until something finally got through to her. The bees. They were flying in a determined manner, the group becoming thicker and thicker. She lifted her head and realized she was witnessing the beginning of a swarm.

Bees were leaving one of the hives, thousands of them flying past her to land on the handle of the same rake she had used to chase the bear away and which still leaned against the other end of the log where she sat.

When she realized what was happening, all thoughts of Caleb and Jacob and the farm fled. She wanted to capture this swarm. These bees came from one of her own hives. She didn't want to let them escape.

The rake handle, she knew, was just a temporary gathering spot, a launch pad for the cluster of bees before they flew off to another temporary spot, from which the scout bees would begin their search for a new location. If she moved fast enough, she could capture the swarm before the scout bees even got busy.

Keeping her movements smooth and unhurried—despite her internal agitation—Rebecca rose, walked out of the bee yard, then gathered her skirts and ran toward the barn. She needed her bee suit as well as a hive box and a couple of frames. Oh, and the bottle of lemongrass oil—that would help direct them into the hive box. She would pile everything into a wheelbarrow and…

She saw Jacob approaching her cabin. When he saw her, he stopped walking. She didn't pause to talk to him, but dashed into the barn, where the beekeeping equipment was kept.

The bee suits were kept in a crate to keep the mice away. Rebecca yanked it open and pulled out her own suit, which she began putting on. She was just zipping up the front zipper when Jacob came in.

"What's up?" he inquired.

"Swarm," she replied shortly.

"Need help?"

She paused. *"Ja."* The forced calmness required when working with the bees would keep her emotions in check. "Can you find the cart or wheelbarrow? I'll pull together the equipment."

He nodded and disappeared, then returned within a minute pushing an empty wheelbarrow. Rebecca nodded her thanks and stacked the hive box, frames, the same cardboard box she'd used with the last swarm, the sheet and bottle of lemongrass oil.

"You might want to get the bee suit on. I'll meet you in the bee yard." She seized the handles of the wheelbarrow and trotted outside.

The bees were still there. The cluster was thicker than before, hanging on the rake handle like a beard. Rebecca pushed the wheelbarrow through the gate of the bee yard and began setting up a hive box on the opposite side of the bee yard from the cluster.

Barely two minutes behind her, Jacob trotted up, his suit zipped up, the bee veil already fastened on, and his elbow-length gloves in place.

"Let me get my veil on." From where it dangled down her back, Rebecca pulled the attached veil over her head and zipped it into place. Then she fitted her own gloves over her hands and up her forearms. "Ready?"

"Ready."

She took the sheet and handed him the cardboard box. Next to the rake, she spread the sheet on the ground, then took the cardboard box and placed it on the sheet. "Let's do this," she muttered. Carefully, she lifted the rake from near its base. The weight of the bees at the upper end was significant, and it took both hands to hold the garden implement while she angled it over the box.

"Here's what I want you to do—take the upper end of the rake," she instructed Jacob. "When I give the word, give it a sharp shake, almost a snap, just once. Just like I did the last time we captured a swarm. *Ja?*"

"Ja."

Through the veil, it was hard to see the expression on his face, but she got the impression he was pleased to play such an active part in the drama.

She maneuvered the rake until the swarm was positioned over the open mouth of the box, then braced herself. "Ready," she told him.

Jacob took the end of the rake handle, gently pushing aside a few bees in the way, then grasped it firmly. "Here goes," he said, and gave the rake a sharp snap downward.

With the same textbook perfection as before, the bulk of the cluster promptly dropped into the box. Jacob gave her a triumphant grin.

She smiled back, remembering the happy time when she had captured her first swarm and the feeling of satisfaction it gave her.

The sound of wings humming increased. Several hundred bees remained clinging to the rake handle. "Give it another jerk," she suggested. "Let's see if we can get most of them in the box."

"Hang on tight, then," he warned. Rebecca re-gripped the lower end of the rake, and Jacob gave the upper end another sharp jolt. Most of the remaining bees dropped into the box, but not all.

"That's probably the best we can do," she said. She

leaned the rake against the T-post again, then kneeled to close the flaps of the box. "It's tempting just to settle the bees into the new hive box right now, but even though it's only a few yards away, I don't want to rush things. I'll wait until evening."

"*Gut.* Then it will give us a chance to talk." Jacob looked at her through the veil.

She felt her midsection clench. "What is there to talk about?"

"Don't be obtuse, Rebecca. There's a *lot* to talk about."

She sighed, knowing he was right. "Let's go to my cabin," she suggested. "I'll make tea."

With Jacob at her side, she walked out of the bee yard, removing her gloves and veil. Jacob did so as well. He said nothing on the way to the cabin. Neither did she. When they got to the small porch of her cabin, they paused to remove the bee suits, then went inside.

"Sit down," she invited. "I'll heat some water."

Jacob dropped into a chair at the kitchen table while she collected mugs, spoons and a bowl of sugar. She placed a basket with a variety of tea bags on the table and let Jacob rifle through them to make his choice.

The kettle seemed slow to heat. Running out of tea accoutrements to fuss with, Rebecca gave up and sat opposite him. "So I gather this caught you as much by surprise as it did me?"

"*Ja*, entirely by surprise." He leveled a look at her. "I hope you don't think I had anything whatever to do with his decision. It was an underhanded thing to do, and I told him as much."

"Gut," snapped Rebecca with asperity. "I feel very betrayed."

"So do I." Jacob rubbed his chin in a gesture of annoyance. "I told him I had uprooted my entire life to move out here with the expectation that I would inherit the farm, and that if he was going to yank the rug from underneath my feet, he could at least have done that before I traveled all this distance."

"I confess, I've been coming up with alternate plans." She toyed with a spoon. "My friend Eva Hostetler has been keeping her ear to the ground, and she told me there's a job available if I want it."

A look of distress swept across Jacob's face. "But I don't want you to go," he blurted out.

"What choice do I have?" She pounded a fist on the table. "For five years, I've filled Caleb's ears with tales of woe regarding my mother's matchmaking efforts. We even had to manufacture a courtship to put off Jeremiah coming all the way out here. And now Caleb pulls this stunt? How could he?"

The kettle started to sing, so she rose and batted off the propane burner with an irritated flick of her hand. She poured hot water into Jacob's mug, then hers.

"So what's the next step?" inquired Jacob, dipping his tea bag up and down in the hot water.

"I don't know." Rebecca slumped in her chair. "I feel so defeated."

"Rebecca…" Jacob pushed away the mug of tea and leaned forward, clasping his hands. They trembled slightly. "Has it occurred to you that you may not have to move?"

"Sure I do."

"*Nein*, you don't."

His eyes were intense. Rebecca stared into their depths, and for some reason her heartbeat quickened. "What are you saying?"

"I'm saying this doesn't have to be a manufactured courtship. It could be a real one."

There. He'd said it. Jacob clasped his hands tightly to stop the slight tremor he couldn't quite control. So much depended on her reaction.

He knew he might have been too blunt, but frankly, he didn't know how to broach the subject except head-on. Besides, Rebecca was not a subtle creature, prone to flattery or flirting or dancing around an issue. She was a woman who appreciated truth and candor.

Into the yawning silence, he pushed on. "Think about it, Rebecca. A genuine courtship would solve both our problems…"

"Or multiply them!" She leaped to her feet and began pacing the kitchen, her skirt swishing in agitation. "Jacob, are you mad? Marriage is forever. We would be yoked the rest of our lives. How can you even entertain such a thought?"

"I'm aware of that." He felt some irritation at her stubbornness. "But, Rebecca, this fear of marriage you have is a phobia. By definition, phobias are irrational. You are a rational, logical woman. It's time you look at the root of your fears and overcome them, rather than spend the rest of your life running and hiding from what your mother did to you."

She looked stunned. "Phobia? You think my aversion to marriage is a phobia?" Abruptly, she sat back down at the table.

"What else can it be? I agree, Caleb's little trick is underhanded, and it pushed me into saying this faster than I wanted. But I was interested in courting you anyway."

"Me? You want to court me? For real?" Her jaw dropped.

His irritation segued into amusement at her utter surprise. "Evidently this comes as a surprise. I thought my changing attitude toward you was apparent, but I guess I was wrong."

"*Ja*, this takes me *completely* by surprise." She buried her face in her hands for a few moments, then lifted her head. "I'm sorry, I didn't see this coming."

A thread of uncertainty ran through him. "Is it your aversion to courtship in general, or is it courtship *from me*?"

"I—I don't know..."

"Well, let me remind you this would be a courtship, not a marriage. At least, not yet. That's what courtship is about, to see if a couple is compatible for marriage. It's not like we'll be standing in front of the bishop next Sunday, after all."

"I...I guess." She gave him a grim smile. "If it's any consolation, I think my aversion is to marriage in general, not necessarily to marriage with *you*."

"Ja gut." He smiled back. "That's helpful to my ego, at least."

He was rewarded with a chuckle. He sensed the worst was over.

Then his curiosity got the better of him. "Were you ever courted by Jeremiah, or were you two just sort of shoved together?"

"Oh, shoved, unquestionably. I think that's why he ran when he did—he didn't want to marry me any more than I wanted to marry him. That's why *Mamm*'s letter that he's back with the church in Indiana and interested in coming out here caught me by surprise. I don't know what happened during his years working in the *Englisch* world, but I can only assume he got disillusioned somehow."

"My guess is most of the women his age are married by now, and the unmarried ones are too young."

"*Ja*, I think you're right. So I'm his last choice." She wrinkled her nose. "Again."

"Now here's another question. Outside of your friend Leah, how many friends or relatives do you know whose marriage is unhappy?"

She was silent a few moments, then shook her head. "No one."

"Why do you think that is?"

"Well, presumably they weren't *shoved* into marriage, for one thing. But—but I guess it's a matter of compatible goals, compatible faith, that kind of thing."

"Faith, family and finances," replied Jacob. "I remember my *mamm* saying that's what needs to be compatible in a marriage. It's simplistic, but there's something to it. So, Rebecca, if you'd accept courtship from me, the odds are in our favor."

"I suppose..." She bit her lip. "So why am I so frightened?"

"Here…" He laid his hands on the table, palms up, in silent invitation. She hesitated a moment, then laid her hands over his.

It was the first time he had ever touched her except that day she'd chased the bear, and the moment was electrifying. He knew she felt it, too, because her eyes widened and her breath quickened.

"Do you think marriage will be so bad?" he whispered.

"Maybe not…" Her words were low.

Still holding her hands, he stood up and pulled her to her feet. Then he looped her arms loosely around his neck and pulled her close for a kiss.

That was all the convincing Jacob needed. He knew the woman in his arms would someday be his wife. Now, if only she felt the same…

After a few minutes, she pulled back. Her eyes were bright. Sparkling, in fact. He could see a pulse pounding in her throat.

"So this is courtship?" She gulped, then smiled.

"*Ja*, I suppose it is." He leaned his forehead against hers. "It's as new to me as it is to you."

"Jacob…there's no guarantee this will lead to marriage, just so you're aware."

"*Ja*, I know that. But I'm willing to leave this in *Gott*'s hands if you are."

She glanced at the clock over the kitchen sink. "We don't have anything to do until this evening, do we? Then we'll have to hive that swarm. Until then…"

His arms tightened around her. "Until then, let's go for a walk. We have a lot to discuss. Besides," he added.

"We're going to have to plant a lot more celery than you're already growing. We may need it."

She chuckled. Hand in hand, they left the cabin.

Epilogue

"I don't know which is more annoying," Rebecca remarked to Jacob. "My *mamm*'s relief or Caleb's smugness. Look at them over there, chatting."

The November morning was crisp but dry. A light dusting of snow lay on the ground as she and Jacob helped with some of the final preparations for their wedding.

Their extended families had arrived a couple days before, ecstatic at the union they were here to witness… *especially* Rebecca's mother.

"I feel sorry for your *mamm* in some ways," teased Jacob. "You're the last of her *kinner* to get married. She's out of children to matchmake. What will she do with her time now?"

"*Ja*, she has a few years before any of my nieces or nephews are old enough to match with anyone." Rebecca grinned. "Maybe I should introduce her to beekeeping."

Jacob burst out laughing. Then, still chuckling, he pulled her into his arms. "I love you."

"*Nein*, you're not fooling me." She stood on tiptoe and planted a kiss on his lips. "You only wanted me for the bees. Admit it."

"The bees were simply a means to an end. I didn't know that at first, but *Gott* did." He made a comical grimace. "And maybe Caleb."

"Funny how he didn't need a *daadi haus* after all. He was happy to swap with me and take over my cabin."

"Caleb is a smart man, and he's already looking forward to grandchildren to dandle on his knee."

"Meanwhile..." Rebecca smiled at her soon-to-be husband and gestured toward the room being set up. "There's enough celery to deck every table. It's a *gut* thing you suggested planting as much as you did."

He grinned back. "Let's just say I had high hopes."

* * * * *

Hash Brown Casserole

Ingredients:

4 lbs. potatoes, grated
½ cup butter, melted
10 oz. can condensed cream of chicken soup
16 oz. sour cream
1 onion, chopped
8 oz. shredded cheddar cheese (about 2 cups)
1 teaspoon salt
½ teaspoon pepper

Directions:

Preheat oven to 375 degrees F.

Grease a 9x13-inch baking dish.

In a large bowl, stir together all of the ingredients until thoroughly combined. Pour into prepared baking dish and bake until golden brown and bubbling, 1.5 to 2 hours. Let rest for 10 minutes before serving.

Dear Reader,

Have you ever resisted the matchmaking efforts of friends or relatives? Being pushed toward someone who doesn't seem suitable is a delicate situation. However, once in a while, the matchmaker knows what she's doing and finds you the perfect match…even if it doesn't seem so at first!

I am fascinated by bees and the science of beekeeping. Sadly, this fascination didn't translate into success when we kept bees on our farm. Writing about Rebecca and her capabilities as a "bee whisperer" almost—but not quite—makes me want to try again.

Like Rebecca, I'm convinced honeybees are one of God's most remarkable creations. However, I think I'll focus on the other aspects of animal husbandry where we've had better success, such as raising cows and chickens.

I hope you found *The Amish Beekeeper's Dilemma* enjoyable. I love hearing from readers, so feel free to email me at patricelewis@protonmail.com.

Blessings,
Patrice

COMING NEXT MONTH FROM **Love Inspired**

AN UNCONVENTIONAL AMISH PAIR

Seven Amish Sisters • by Emma Miller

When her employer's son returns after an eight-year absence, Henrietta Koffman fears she'll lose her handywoman job—but ends up with a helper instead. As they work together, neither can deny the attraction or the underlying problem—Chandler Gingerich isn't Amish. With a little faith, can an unlikely pair become a perfect match?

THE AMISH BAKER'S SECRET COURTSHIP

by Amy Grochowski

Opening a bakery has always been Cassie Weaver's dream—one that hinges on her good friend Martin Beiler. Now Martin's home to fulfill his promise to help set up her bakeshop. But when everyone suspects they're secretly dating, will their pretend courtship begin to feel like more?

BONDING WITH THE BABIES

K-9 Companions • by Deb Kastner

After she rejected his public proposal, Frost Winslow never thought he'd see Zoey Lane again—until she walks back into his life with their twin babies. Now they're learning how to be parents together and starting over. But a real family could be in their future...if Zoey makes peace with her past.

HIS UNEXPECTED GRANDCHILD

by Myra Johnson

Lane Bromley is shocked when he learns he has a grandson. Now he's caring for the little boy—except his paternal grandmother, veterinarian Julia Frasier, thinks the child belongs with *her*. But finding a compromise is one thing. Accidentally finding love is quite another...

THE COWBOY'S RETURN

Shepherd's Creek • by Danica Favorite

Leaving his troubled past behind, Luke Christianson returns to his hometown to care for his grandmother—and discovers he's a father. As he gets to know his teenage daughter, Luke and Maddie Anter, the mother of his child, grow closer. Will a family conflict stand in the way of their happily-ever-after?

A FATHER'S VOW

by Chris Maday Schmidt

Dedicated to protecting his daughter and hometown, widower Constable Jack Wells will do anything to stop the vandalism at their beloved wildlife preserve—even partner with its new veterinarian. Soon their on-duty stakeouts evolve into off-duty family outings. But with heartbreak in their pasts, are they ready to risk a second chance?

LOOK FOR THESE AND OTHER LOVE INSPIRED BOOKS WHEREVER BOOKS ARE SOLD, INCLUDING MOST BOOKSTORES, SUPERMARKETS, DISCOUNT STORES AND DRUGSTORES.

LICNM0224